PASSES THROUGH

PASSES THROUGH

Rob Stephenson

introduction by Lance Olsen

FC2

TUSCALOOSA

The University of Alabama Press
Tuscaloosa, Alabama 35487-0380

Published by FC2, an imprint of the University of Alabama Press, with support provided by the Publications Unit of the Department of English at Illinois State University, and the School of Arts and Sciences, University of Houston–Victoria

Address all editorial inquiries to: Fiction Collective Two, University of Houston–Victoria, School of Arts and Sciences, Victoria, TX 77901-5731

⊗

The paper on which this book is printed meets the minimum requirements of American National Standard for Information Sciences—Permanence of Paper for Printed Library Materials, ANSI Z39.48–1984

Library of Congress Cataloging-in-Publication Data
Stephenson, Rob, 1967-
Passes through / Rob Stephenson; introduction by Lance Olsen. — 1st ed.
   p. cm.
ISBN-13: 978-1-57366-155-3 (pbk. : alk. paper)
ISBN-13: 978-1-57366-817-0 (ebook)
1. Psychological fiction. I. Title.
PS3619.T47693P37 2010
813'.6—dc22

                              2009038682

Book Design: Jason Werwie and Tara Reeser
Cover Design: Lou Robinson
Typeface: Baskerville
Produced and printed in the United States of America

Passes Through ::: Passing For ::: Not Knowing
Lance Olsen

Rob Stephenson's *Passes Through* is the opposite of an easy or fun book, at least by current Oprah-ized standards. It is, rather, a limit text—one that takes writing to the edge of readability, then challenges us to invent new ways to speak about its strangeness. That is, it's a text about textual and epistemological boundaries, a narrative that refuses predictable narrativity even while advancing our ideas about narratology, a meticulous exercise in the denial of conventional modes of coherence. Its sometimes flat and sometimes jagged prose, its density, the diligent line-by-line labor it requires of its readers evinces nothing if not what I think of as the Difficult Imagination: the sort interested in involved, nuanced fictions dedicated in heterodox ways to confronting, interrogating, complicating, and even for brief periods of time short-circuiting those McDonaldized narratives produced by the dominant cultures that would like to see their stories told and retold until they begin to pass for something like "truths" about the human condition. Which is to say: *Passes Though* invites us to partake of Viktor Shklovsky's ambition for art, Martin Heidegger's for philosophy: the return, through complexity and challenge, to perception and contemplation.

To generate the book in your hands, Stephenson four times "passed through" the journal he kept for ten years, erasing many lines and passages, rearranging others, appropriating and manipulating shards from found texts along the way. As he explained in a recent letter: "I have passed through my journal and passed many things through it and the journal has passed back through me and the many things. I have made fiction out of the fiction I found there." The result is a conceptual language collage divided into three sections (each with its own series of guiding constraints) that enacts literally Barthes's contention that a text is "a multi-dimensional space in which a variety of writings, none of them original, blend and clash. The text is a tissue of quotations drawn from the innumerable centers of culture." Within *Passes Through*'s pages, we find no real plot, no full character, no full scene, not even many paragraphs or much white space—nothing, that is, aimed at helping us orient in ways we are used to orienting as we settle into a new fiction. Instead, we discover a protean consciousness obsessing over art, food, writing, the nature of language, the grammar of relationships, S&M, gay erotica, selfhood's slippage.

That final fixation—selfhood's slippage—leads us to two of the *Passes Through*'s central thematics and problematics. First, Stephenson's is a book shot through with an awareness of Henri Bergson's pivotal idea from *Matter and Memory*: that we cannot experience the present, since it is always-already something other than the present by the time we have processed it and made it (or, better, tried to make it) our own; that at best to be alive is to experience a relentlessly ongoing expression of the past tense, or, more to the point, particles of "pastness" that we may or may not be remembering (something like) accurately. Second, *Passes Through* is a book, not unlike Michael Joyce's *Was*, or, in a different key, Ben Marcus's *The Age of Wire and String* or *Notable American Women*, that presses against the prose poem's form as it considers mnemonic overload both at a personal and cultural stratum. (Actually, the implication here is that there is very little difference, if any, between the two.)

At the end of the day, however, it strikes me that Stephenson's text may be less involved in avant-garde literary conversations than in avant-garde musical ones. Stephenson himself, for instance, has collaborated with Mikael Karlsson on the CD *dog*, eleven sound collages which fuse contemporary classical composition with improvisation, spoken word, and the deliberate misuse of hardware and software. When I try to imagine aesthetic antecedents for *Passes Through*, what comes to mind most readily are Karlheinz Stockhausen's and John Cage's atonal, aleatoric investigations of serial composition. What comes to mind are Morton Feldman's slow, repetitive, rhythmically irregular whispers in which chords arrive in what strikes the ear as haphazard sequences continuously hovering between consonance and dissonance. (It's not for nothing that one of Feldman's most well-known works is *Rothko Chapel*.) What comes to mind is the anecdote about how, after a group of musicians did their best to edge through one of Feldman's scores as softly as humanly possible, the brash composer snapped: "It's too fuckin' loud, and it's too fuckin' fast!" What comes to mind is Feldman's assertion that what was so great about the Fifties was that "for one brief moment—maybe, say, six weeks—nobody understood art."

(At the beginning of this decade, all writers should be so lucky.)

What comes to mind is Feldman's famous council: "Just concentrate on not making the lazy move."

There is nothing lazy here. What we find in what follows is a painstaking study into compositional processes and systems, into what writing is and what it can be. Another way of saying this is that in addition to Stephenson's text *passing through* notions of intertextuality, avant-musicality, recollection and re-collection, it also *passes for* a novel. And yet it isn't a novel. And yet it is. Or, rather, it is a text that tests us about what a novel might be by presenting us with what one isn't… quite. Perhaps we can talk about this narratological queering as a critifiction (to appropriate and reconfigure Raymond Federman's provocative term): a mode of discourse suspended between two sorts of imagination, one theoretical and one creative. But that, as well, seems a little too easy a conceptual hotel in which to room such an invigorating, frustrating, elusive, cerebral, sad, surprising, liberating, unfamiliar work whose every measure reminds us that the word *narrative* is ultimately derived from the Proto-Indo-European root *gno*, within which echoes our own verb *know*: to make sense, to understand, to apprehend with clarity and certainty—which is the opposite, or nearly the opposite, of what *Passes Through* attempts.

What comes to mind, in the end, then, is Donald Barthelme's resonant pronouncement concerning fiction's present (and, I would like to think, care to wager, Fiction Collective Two's future): "Art is not difficult because it wishes to be difficult, rather because it wishes to be art. However much the writer might long to be straight-forward, this virtue is no longer available to him…. Writing is a process of dealing with not-knowing."

DYAD

Everything happens as though our recollections were repeated an infinite number of times in these many possible reductions of our past life. They take a more common form when memory shrinks most, more personal when it widens out, and they thus enter into an unlimited number of different systematizations.

Henri Bergson —*Matter and Memory*

I'm the gap between what I'd like to be and what others have made me.

Fernando Pessoa writing as Álvaro de Campos

…when I sleep my brow is as smooth as that of my double.

Vladimir Nabokov —*Despair*

one

No one could stay in the gallery for more than five minutes. The heat and humidity were merciless. I was still collecting pictures. I would look at two of the photographs and go back out into the rain. I went in and out five times. Outside, I stood on the curb. I am always standing on the edge. Never pulled in for long. I can't be pulled into the center. There were newspapers arranged by topic and tucked into folders. Everything old and reused. Lovers on a bed. Chairs everywhere. Blood and anger. The bodies completely asexual. They came from a time when sex and magic were connected in people's minds. Red. Red. Red. Circles within ellipses. Not enough thinking about thinking. The strategy of drawing in piecemeal. Even the landscapes were on a budget, as if they were wallpaper. Everything subdued. All this sits in my guts as I write, making my regimen soft. He had this rare opportunity to focus on a part of life most of the population was trying not to think about. He talked about their glorious empire of fear, the wonder of their ingenious war machines, and their gods' love of bloodshed. A drunken king reclines with his queen. Attendants fan them. The heads of his enemies are hung from nearby trees. He emitted the scent of boldness and decay. The white clothesline looked good against his skin. His balls hung so low I wound the rope seven times around the wrinkled skin above them. Rodeo horses with their testicles tied tight to make them bucking broncos. But he was quiet and adorable for a few seconds. I miss that kind of intimacy. We made a scene in the grocery store. Gummy bears. The struggle for power and identity. Spun around by the forces of attraction and repulsion. Two magnets hanging on strings. Two cats staying in separate rooms. Wary of how story and design shape each other. Not ready to get along. No one sleeps. Afterwards, a small but significant reversal. He wins by a hair. I am appalled. For a minute I thought he was going to get out his ruler. Home becomes uncomfortable. There is no air. There is no center left except for what I've imagined inside of me. Only when I'm traveling can I find that center.

Initially, I felt this story was encompassing too many ideas. I keep changing as I go. I had hoped to stay true in some sense to what I started. But then I began to wonder if a writer's instincts should be disregarded. Maybe I should let them go.

These little documents of my personal moments. Should I be writing down my everyday thoughts? The ones that don't strike me as important. The invisible repetitions. The underlying pitter pats. The recollections of corresponding numbers on the face of an irrelevant clock. I continue to find beauty in unusual places. Some of which are still unspeakable. Blurry edges. Wonderful images that sit in the mind. Made rich by the variegated detail retained and amplified by review. Art should have enough layers of meaning so that you can come back to it over and over again and find new things. But muddled things are not the same as things that have depth or multiple meanings. None of this is news. Some art you can appreciate better when you've acquired a certain way of seeing. Learning another language so you can translate it back into your own. A stasis in the interval. Secrets that stay underneath. In the dark. Stay beyond the corruption of analysis. It is the hidden things that drive him on. A fuel that works in tandem with the part that is not out there in the open. A long side. Parallels make a fiction that reminds him to live. There is life beyond the rhythmic impulses of key tapping. I let a character think something he really didn't have the capacity to think. But then again, imperfect objects may become catalysts. He was high in every scene and knew where he was in the world. He returned again and again to a particular place. A calm reverie prior to traumatic experience. I disliked the oversized parrot that talks to him and runs his spaceship. He said he was into the new age religions. I said I would slap the gods right out of him. I lose interest as soon as they appear. That is my own bias. I must be the most contaminated sign in my own language. Maybe that's a shortcut to the sacred. Light bulbs in a circle behind the images. Not just an ordinary flower can take on implausible aesthetic radiance. So tall and skinny. Big fucking fingers point to the sky. Black sweatshirt with a burning skull on it. Shaved head. Wing tattoos inked on the back of it. Cryptic squiggles dip under his shirt and ride down the ridge of his spine. Taciturn features. High-tech cropped goatee. Kiss. He's too drunk. Kiss again. Damn. What is so great about not knowing what country you're in at the moment? The gods are all and everywhere he said. In that sunset over there and in your shit. They derive a peculiar pleasure when they pass through unrecognized. At the end of an episode, life has lost its ongoing character. Our perception of succession it seems is dependent on the possibilities of organization.

I sat down at a table with an older man. Macaroni and cheese. He lived nearby. A tall young man sat down next to him. Peach cobbler. The fattest thumbs I'd seen in ages. The older man spoke of how he had killed chickens at summer camp. A broom handle on the neck. A foot on either end. Jerking the body back to snap the head off. Oh ick said the young man. The old man said there was a baby calf that he named and adopted. It became dinner at some point. The young man interrupted to ask him if he'd eaten it. The old man wasn't sure, but said he should have spent more energy on the camp counselors. I said that could lead to a lifetime of cannibalism. The older man said he always enjoys what he eats and stared at the young man. I get the urge to destroy things. I bite my knuckles instead. I stuff myself into pockets of rage. The smallest movement triggers it. Walks along the boulevard. Lilacs, dogwoods, tulips. It's crucial to determine how each one manifests itself. Mostly, the voices are supportive, even witty. Occasionally, they are cruel. They swear and tell him to hurt himself. It's funny, the different ways people protect their personal space. I was never at home there in his place. One time he put on the coat his mother had sent him. Inside out. We laughed until we were sore. Some little rapture. And them some more. I dragged him outside in his underwear. Night-blooming jasmine. The first summer rain on hot pavement. Strange isolated moments. Equal children. Boys again. Enjoying the boy things together. Sweet fleeting peace. Two lilies sticking it out in a field of weeds. And then the corny way he channeled a room full of famous fucked-up women. It had a cantankerous charm. Tough bitches who've seen the wars. The inner wars. Different from mine. The pills helped him manage but he never eradicated them. He wore the wounds inside out, too. Hollow treats bounced around and burst open on our faces. The favorite old-time cosmetic covered our hands. Reeking of violets. It made us cackle. We fought and said it was the fault of the other. The part that aims too high can count the losses. He hears the voices of strangers. Chaotic and irrepressible. They told him all tears are selfish. What goes on between people anyway? I always find beauty in horrible things. The way comedians talk about mothers-in-law. An inescapable part of life and you must adjust to it. Did you get a pet? Do you think about me? Silence gets wider and wider. Safety first. Yes, an internet agreement about silence. Countersigned in silence. And then there are hobbies. Regular visits to the library. Honing those computer skills. He made birds out of typing paper. Desperate for someone to waste time with. He never wrote in his notebook. But I began to use language to express something closer to how I really think. I left things out. I merged others together in odd configurations that are lost when I try to recapture them now. Sleepy boy. Nose in a dictionary. A fount of knowledge. Cutting each description into thin rectangles. Spreading them across the table. Face down. Why is it that I pander at all to the reader?

I was filled with regret today. Ghosts are everywhere. I feel more and more like a fool. It is such a sorrowful thing. Losing the ability to see a person in a positive light. What you desire greatly begins to show up around you in little pieces until you see it everywhere. It points right at you wherever you are. He mentioned he was no longer interested in architecture or lovely furniture. I feel as if I'm outside the whole interaction. I watch him talk to me, but his words are a mantra to keep him tuned to the incredibly small world necessary for his security. The world of the absolute answers to everything. The same songs over and over. The world I run from every day. I am not sure how to make plans for us to do things together. I am no longer certain of what will offend him. He looked amused at that. His sentimentality is heartless. Everything must fit into an order that at all costs will be maintained. Rude characterizations are artificially stamped on every character. There are bound to be unpleasant consequences. I feel guilty because it was easy for a while. I am a shadow. A senseless road. That's what he said. My life is a hesitation. I type. He drifts. The rudder is stuck on this boat. He doesn't need both hands. We were served a meal where one peppered dish after another burned a different region of the mouth and throat. What answers do I think I need from him? I feel the wild tempo of the inner process. Useless patterns. Unsettled. Brittle. Our clocks are not in unison.

There is some taking that is not given willingly. There are degrees of rape that transport what is seen into something else, something unaware. What parts of me do you want? I'm all twisted together in a tangle. The idea of collecting myself includes untruths I no longer even know about until they come to the surface. Balancing a clinically maintained self with a passionate driven self. Where can I take this? What is the best way to expand this character? To what end? I settled for watching a movie with him. Roughly filmed and edited with a jagged elegant economy. It was about whether a man is a factory or a landscape. There was a landscape and they built a factory on it. There was a factory and they put a landscape around it. He thought the character didn't speak from inside his own script, but with the words someone else gave him. A mirage born of despair. He knew how to be a bastard and come out looking pretty good. And he wanted revenge against a way of thinking that buries the deepest thoughts inside a secret place. You trust yourself too much, you pretending piece of self-deprecating sponge.

That museum is overwhelming. Too much private desire in a public place. I particularly enjoyed the barbed wire collection. Over one hundred varieties. Lengths of it radiating out and around a large oval frame. Inside it was an old photograph. Sepia-toned. Horns and antlers. Particles of dust. Dirt that attaches itself to a car. Fibers from his clothes. The procession of insects that arrive at the dead body in a predicable and datable sequence. I wonder if addictive behavior manifests itself the same way in countries with different religious emphases. I would like to find those dangerous old visions. To love the forbidden things that could be found without much effort in the library. He suggested a whole new set of moves through a pair of thick brooding lips. He had the cheapest tickets. Secret thrills that were better than the ones the other kids were looking for outside in their cars. I feel so selfish. He must think I'm an animal. Real noise directs us away from the message itself toward the medium in which it occurs. I have to get away from this city. Avoid the same traps. These awful feelings of ruin. Such mediocre stuff. It turns out each middle has its own distinct properties that affect the message in precise ways. Shut up and fill in the gaps with something multifaceted. Will we see the end of his bad ideas about love?

He has a way of making everything I do seem unimportant. I don't think he means it. But sometimes I just want to have an ego. The problem of owning instead of renting. I like it when he calls me daddy. When he thinks I make all the right decisions. Even when I'm wrong. I like getting the praise I don't deserve. When I steal the glory. I've entered a game where I suddenly become this person that's a different person from the one you've been speaking to. I excel in this highly organized form of pretending. Capable of dastardly behavior. The gradual reintroduction of their ideas into my own. I know the jokes, the references to all kinds of old art. It's an odd use of the dead. The vanished. There is always continuity. Maybe everything has already vanished. Not much physical evidence left. Objects can be irrelevant. They don't pre-exist in a valuable state. And still I've spent so much of my life trying to make usable structures. Everything is contaminated. I'm not sure how to proceed. To find better definitions. It's futile to have a part of your life that no one can touch. The limbo between prose and poetry.

Someone else's right thing. Lots of military guys. Standing there. Guarding emptiness. People are taking photographs in groups. Parasitic tourists. He says I am experiencing the accumulated charred and unholy ends of all my failed relationships. Boy, I do hate lazy reviewers.

Don't listen to that. Hold back a little. Save something for yourself. Save yourself. Don't let them take it away again and again. They can separate you into segments and lay them down side by side. In the shadowless light. I've been tired of living, but not tired enough to finish the job. To lose every reason to stay. Keep everything in the same pervasive darkness. You have to believe that feeling nothing is an improvement. There is a great wall that I helped him build. I didn't have enough tenderness. I sat silent on a wooden chair. Devising it all. Unwilling to start the little games again. I have kept some of the most precious things he gave me. I wanted to see his tears. He was just life babbling a bubble bath. Bursting with good intentions. More and more. With every inane word the evidence of the past crinkles up in my own mind. What could be worse than a cold asshole? My kaleidoscope of experience was more beautiful than I wanted it to be. Adjustable as in the case of certain piano stools. I will choose the new words more carefully and watch them become part of the wall. What can you do with what you've done? Why do you do anything at all? But you keep doing it just the same. You see people and scream at them, but they don't hear anything. So you settle for a more subtle approach, like writing perhaps. In the store I saw an illustration of a man with long red hair. His coat had dozens of pieces of paper fixed to it. Each paper had words on it. The foundation pins from the first city were shaped like people. Words were carved into their garments. No one says those names anymore. They held up walls. I think of the words I've been writing. Will these ancient words, these names ever be spoken again? And could anyone understand their original meaning? Words like these. Not the same words. Came from me before. And came from somewhere else. Long ago. I wanted them to be transparent so there would never be misunderstanding again. I wanted to make them unchangeable. But I didn't buy the card. I left the store and the whole idea of wanting to preserve exactness in language. I let the words change and let them change me. There was no choice really. We had sea bass for dinner at quarter to eight. I slept on his mother's single bed. The mattresses were covered in plastic. Every time I turned over the bedding slid onto the floor. There was a nice view of the ocean. The tide comes inside me and goes back out again. It leaves little slimy things. It smoothes the fragments I pick up or stumble over. It doesn't matter what I do with them. They come and go. Like everything. Chipping away at all the old worlds, the old words, the different names that make up great walls. These barriers I forget to unbuild. Someone high or drunk does not feel nothing. They feel differently. Numb, perhaps. But something. History makes me numb. It's so tall I can't see over it. It makes me want to kill this world, but the only way to do that is to kill myself. Those old words kill me slowly in painful frustrating ways. I can't take the old words away. I can only add to them. I can't understand them either. They are all fused together. Layered into undecipherable blackness. An imperfect dark. The great wall. And then I realized the new words that I thought were chipping away at the wall are slowly becoming the same old wall and maybe they were part of the wall from the start. I'm just moving them around. And that's all there is to do. After so many words.

A big house in a row of big houses surrounded by rows of other big houses. Our room had an old radio built into the bed. Punk rock blared from one tinny speaker. The bed had twenty little pillows on it. Each one a unique size and shape. Words sewn on them in a flowery script. He gathered them together like stones. A couple of gin and tonics. A half-eaten sandwich. The kitchen light. The lumpy mattress. This small infidelity. An exhilarated me. His lovely accent. A joint burning in the ashtray. The dirty yellow linoleum between his legs. Just another perverted stranger. Gorgeous and unsolvable. I'm farther away at each successive moment. The illusions he caters to are so different from mine. Somewhere the cops are still bending that kid over the trunk of his car. One stands directly behind him. The kid's pants riding low on his butt. A fortuitously aimed flashlight. I see two inches of his crack. They hit him with boards. Just a few feet from me. I am electrified by my proximity to the violent act. They see me and make a show out of it until I move away. Behind an abandoned cage on the sidewalk. Rusted into some kind of monument. A temple, perhaps. For small animals. I sat on one of the huge stones lying on its side nearby. The tourists kept silent as they passed through my reflection. I envisioned kings and princes frolicking with each other among a muster of peacocks. I wake up next to yet another exquisite creature. We have lox and bagels with cream cheese and cucumbers. There are always leftovers in a relationship whose boundaries are never in plain view. The mind stutters. Too many different trains of thought in such a short time. Holding onto each other. Never a convincing conclusion in a graying countryside. By sundown we've collected many theories of why. If only I could photograph them. But it's always so blurry after the verbal parts.

The work place is a disappointment with its rigidly drawn lines. Taking risks is important for me. That way I feel as if I'm advancing. I hate being the one who has to wait for everything. This patriotism is exasperating, but I enjoyed the idea of saving the world with a laptop. Now we are looking in the guidebooks. I can't hear the unspoken thoughts in his head, but I can feel him moving through the motions of speech. You have to swim in it. Spend time in the deep end. There are limits to what can be said. A sequence unfolds as a succession of states. Each state becomes a moment frozen in time. A snapshot that the mind's eye can't see unaided. If you lay one language on top of another one, they don't cover the same area. And they don't extend infinitely in any direction. At this point I decided he was yet another blank-faced hero, more suited to collecting glances in cafes and subway stations or for passing messages in the dark without making a sound. I told him I'd thrown out that old sofa. He said he liked it and what we'd done on it. He drove me at dizzying speeds through the hills outside the city. His sports car followed a number of optional but predetermined routes. We spun out and almost went over the edge. I think I'm an elitist. I wanted his night writing twisting around inside me. Each movement corresponding to a letter from a secret alphabet. What if you only had one memory you could keep? I live in a sea of them. They exhibit barnacle-like tendencies. I've learned to scrape my hull every so often, but there are always some icky parts hanging around. It is my business to squeeze these lumps back into fluid. Parallel lines never form a ladder. The very nature of fundamentalism is exclusionary. He describes a terrible situation as a child. Raised by parents who tried to force an exterior personality on him. He made a remarkable incense burner shaped like a ball and rolled it across plush carpets to scent them. An ongoing music for noses. The residue of a possible answer. Slightly morbid and more beautiful than the last smile of the oldest whore in town.

He repeated the same ten phrases over and over again. I was lying beside him fully dressed. I felt his heat through the blankets. I listened to him sleeping and laughed because he was slurring his words. The impossibility of a relationship is what attracts me. It lies beneath the threshold of awareness. Showing vulnerability never works. He says when your parents are dead, things get easier. They live for years and years. A few practiced stories coming out of their heads. You hear them when they come to visit. He says there must be millions of them buried inside, but only the same dreary tales are trotted out on schedule. I am throwing two folded pieces of paper into the night air. Over and over again. One says go. The other says don't go. He only speaks when he's dreaming. Otherwise, it's as if he's lost his vocabulary. He says he's more damaged than he actually is. He could be my undoing. Sometimes he starts to give an original answer, but it changes into gibberish or one of the ten phrases. Once, when I asked him how he was doing, he said he was always terrified. I don't like repeating bad behavior. I can't deal with the repercussions. I can't afford it anymore. When you're away, I have to go on reading all of those books you've talked about and listen to all the songs you like over and over again. I might be able to figure out what you're feeling. I want to find the words that entered you and stuck there. He spreads two fingers apart and points to his eyes, then extends his hand, palm down, and wiggles it in an undulating motion. He holds up three fingers. Voices rise on top of each other. Each one trying harder to be heard than the next. I think it's just a gimmick. He says how things are in the world makes a difference in my actions, but the sorting mechanism becomes a curse. I want some unified system I can comprehend. He says pictures aren't for measuring. They just go inside. I suspect he has a procedure for demolishing someone's confidence. My concern is the amount of light that passes through. When I am alone. I only have insides.

He avoids thinking with the same gusto that I pursue it. His unshaven face helps me lead an intentional life. Otherwise I am a shadow. A separated moment. A diversion. A still plaything for myself. It's a tight fit. But he manages. What part of me feels like I can't move? I rest inside a boundary I call reality. But I sit just on the other side of it. Making a wall. Trying to bring a wall down. Stone by stone. Shutting out. Letting in. Semi-permeable membrane. Quite a wonderful display. Individual pages are mounted between glass. You can view them from either side. They are lit for only one minute out of five. There's no chance for the damage that comes from continual exposure. The computer stations are full of my unwillingness. Funny beliefs. Letters of acceptance. He told me his despair was from being misunderstood. It involved another person. Whereas mine was only about myself. He said he was no longer interested in architecture or deadlines. Now there's a loaded word. Timing is everything. Library books are overdue. He's still trying to figure out which character is going to kick the bucket. I told him their eyes are different from ours. Someone has created obstacle courses for their couriers. Carriers of their ideas. It's the fine art of positioning them in such a way that they can activate themselves by rubbing up against new elements. Each day's a new day. There's always more weather. But it isn't fresh or original. It's two-day old left on the sidewalk soap opera crap. I thought I would try to skip all that this time around. I have to get offline and get my character to deny his exclusive relationship with the world. Leaving him to himself is often the best punishment. Rough handling doesn't seem to deter him. Behind him hangs a little bucket full of rotting flesh. There is no axe to grind. No escape hatch. The frozen sea has melted into a muddy puddle. As it turns out, death is perhaps unwittingly apt.

I am going to schedule time. To write as I always wanted. The most difficult thing in the world to do. I need to formulate the questions. Even out the hours of writing within the city. Every day warrants some kind of reportage. Yet I feel more and more distant from things around me. I run to the inner world to interpret the outer one. These days the difference between the two is negotiable. I look at everything wondering what I should throw out. Maybe it's the medication. He likes to arrange things. His schema can be considered a network. A grid. What occurs in one region awakens echoes in others. One ends up with a model in order to link all these different points in time and space. I told him I needed to be liked for my uniqueness. He said I should think more about that. An hour goes so slowly when someone is talking. I imagined chance meetings with him where I punch him until he cries. He told me playacting allows us to be what we aren't supposed to be. He was always getting the dirty end of the stick. He's still depressed because he says there is nothing to be done. Margaritas and nachos for every meal. Sitting upstairs in the bar. Looking at the insects pinned to the wall and who knows what else. Hate me. I'm different now. Can we start again? It wasn't just my fault. Why don't you say something I haven't already heard? You look at me funny. I see the wall I helped you build. Do you want my new number? I'm all grown up finally. It's an endless chain of typographic fantasies. That's why it is so difficult to know what's happening to him. There are so many historical layers and swells, because I am obliged to bring in elements that are from outside. So in some ways it looks like another dense and consuming read. Beware the smell of buttered popcorn and cowboys.

You squirm a little. A cocoon of tires. Your position implies penetration into the body by a foreign thing. You're pressed back against the fence. Held in place by a series of metal clamps that encircle your ankles, wrists, waist, and neck. The rubber that encases you makes you sweat continuously. I want to feel you from behind with my hand. Just to frustrate you even more. Instead I enjoy the idea that any attention at all would give you more pleasure than it would me. It is the absence of my touch that pushes you further along. I like that I can make you nervous, yet I want you to trust me. That's the most important thing. How long this time? Ten minutes in this bright moonlight. Fifteen? Thirty? You realize we are not alone in this park. As each minute passes you become more convinced they are watching you. There are always a few of them in the shadows under the oak trees that line the perimeter of the baseball diamond. A dog barks. Your gag is fully inflated, pressing on all the surfaces inside your mouth. Your loudest scream would sound like a pigeon trilling. You jerk your head around. I know rivers of sweat are running down your body into your boots. The words of a corporate super-nanny interfere with mine. You aren't even looking at me anymore. I'm trying to write this with the television bleating. Everybody complains about the impossibility of finding the right text. A sputtering object holds my attention. Its throat cut. Can voices be silenced by considering only exteriors and surfaces?

The sex toys are all clean. Cold and lovely on the wall. No more quiet corners left for us. The need to find something else on my plate. Maple sugar and bean sprouts. In the middle of nowhere. Finding that book in the stacks. Paragraphs cut out. I still look for that box of colored pencils you gave me. And still thoughts. At dinner. Sharpened montages come at a mind wanting sleep. Around and around the same spiraling loop. Strings of fireworks fizzle and explode in whirling wheels of sulfur. Discarded adjectives linger. More traffic noise. The competition of every headline to leave its trace. The lights from speeding cars. Too many words trying to describe a small detail. We waited for a taxi and saw a symmetrically smashed rat in the gutter. The rainwater gushed over it. He sketched hostile trees on top of my pages. Already thick with words. My own anger settled into an uncomfortable detachment. I can't hate him for his confusion. I can only move away from it. Avoiding the same traps. Changing the long-term result of feelings. Understandably, he is looking for a place where he cannot be touched. He's not even sure who he is supposed to be in this story. I need to reach a different audience. I need a more blinding light. To learn how to undo what is made of all the old words. He said the only way to kill the self is to make a new world. The old words weaken you slowly. However, I continue on. Maybe it's time to start rereading what I've written here. But I'm afraid whole passages are being lost at every moment. I can't bear it really. He is, of course, stuck on the page where I left him. A malignant shadow of something that once was.

The need to be with someone is so persistent. The turgid pith of wilting plants. I need someone to be a mirror. But not to look like me. They have to be different so they can reflect me in a highly personalized distortion. Tension is useful. And simple to make. We played cards for money. Apple stems and the tendons of human hands. I envy his ability to make complexity meaningful. Not simple-minded either. Ideas are recalled, rethought. Rerouted into strands. Rewoven into a sinewy mat that sits before the most intimidating portal imaginable. Ghosts are everywhere. They lurk near every opening. Waiting for stitches to break. A wound is a doorway for indistinct impressions. Shapeless masses that seek a body. Structure clarifies things in the immediate vicinity. The best reintegration forms an inexact composite. A feeble map constructed. A piece of cloth has little interest for me until I know whether it is starched, hand woven, salmon pink, knotted, torn, bespangled, or sodden. He was clipped out of an intricate essay in favor of reader abuse. Some days

I miss the space he filled. And the one I filled in him. Forever playing the same song over and over, until I made a nasty retort. I never missed a day writing this journal. Even when his song stopped. I could hear the lies piling up. A tinkling inventory stretching in all directions. Lines of colored powder to put in a birch box he gave me. Four drawings. One on each side. The leaf of the tobacco plant. The wing of a bat. The breastplate of a turtle. The jawbone of an ass. He kept talking about ruins, which ones I should see when I traveled. I told him I was interested in all versions of history. Especially the wrong ones. The fictional aspects. Absurd inventions that fill those big gaps. I found moths in the flour. Flies against the kitchen windowpanes. Finally, I wanted to be back in the library. Watching dark men studying. Reading about ziggurats and the elegant tensile cords made from spiders' silk. It was there that I learned the role of pressure in maintaining the precise shape necessary for sharp vision.

The joke is on me. He never received my letter. The one I regretted sending him. As if I sent it every hour. So I never called him. His checks were stolen the same day. Right out of his mailbox. My handwriting was differently sloped then. A game of hide and seek. Things happen. Good and bad things. Flattened into a pancake. Twinges of remorse and rejection over the absence of a phone call. The process of undermining gets out of hand on television. I spent the better part of nights just waiting for the bell. It's theater for me. Not affectionate or caring in itself. Reflected in his melancholy logic. His insight into nightmares. Bleeding into the years ahead. Coloring everything in my circle. Our fortress of identity divided against itself. A little shadow that goes in and out with me. A no-no. An object without a mask. Better things to do. Push on with the searching. Always searching. The higher purpose. The elevated state of mind. Isn't that exactly what I ran away from in the beginning? Those redundant aims for improvement.

For a time, I was not allowed to exist as myself. I was hidden inside a structure that kept me in a constant state of fear. Restricted to contours. Tell the dream from that perspective. Tell me what it is like to wait without being able to move. Well, not much of a plot, but nice character development. Summer rain. Thunder and lightning. Playing cards. Dark chocolate poured over vanilla ice cream. A certain distance. Three messages on my machine. Animal, vegetable, or mineral. Everything is contaminated. So the world is accused of complicity. Those old patterns of longing. A piece caught in the throat can be neither accepted nor rejected. We did a tail-chasing kind of dance. Beautiful and risky as we fell into an abyss together at the same speed. You and me outside in the parking lot. In the dead of night. It was as though I had never seen black, but was unable to stop imagining that it was something beyond all colors. You were wearing a form-fitting latex cat suit. Lubed up and sweaty. Hidden from sight by your favorite fraying running suit. You were cuffed to a cyclone fence with your arms fully extended out from your torso. Gagged with your own stinking red socks. Looking down at my boots. They were covered with a fine layer of dust. The full moon just emerging from behind the clouds. Color changes and changes me. Therefore it is alive. I should learn to consider the paths of others even when they don't intersect with mine. I severed your arms and put them in a black waterproof bag. I felt the world collapse. A deflating balloon that empties itself of all meaning. All analogies are equally dangerous. But inevitable. In time they become so heavily insistent that objects start to waver. To give way. They melt together in the mind. Despite everything, vision remains our best weapon.

I'm still pissed. Even after coming up from the long sleep. Waiting for vicious feeling to subside. The cunning skein of his late tale. It's torture to have a feeling like that holding all the other ones in place. Watching a slow death is one way to learn the inner equipment of men. He wears a nice linen suit, but underneath he twitches in his lacy black panties. I see the rounded sentences collecting and fully expanding their breaths. What passes for restraint is usually pure deception. A profit making concern. Luke-warm measures. Apple pie. A stratagem of incremental repetitions. The shifting play of thoughts and images is unfathomable. It is not vivid details alone that make artistry. I favor the empty stream. A great silence. An impenetrable forest. The absence of joy in the brilliance of sunshine. Two cats staying in separate rooms. Not ready to get along. He refused to weaken his story by introducing irrelevancies. But I think everything he says is irrelevant and therefore important. This is how time advances and withdraws as in a succession of long dark waves. The roar of the tide reflected in the babble of voices. He used to drive me at dizzying speeds alongside long curving stretches of untamed jungle. Now, he just talks about trains.

In the room there were two beds, two bedside tables, two tanks of oxygen. The door divided the space into two equal sides, each with an identical window. He arranged to have candy bars hidden in progressively remote locations. That way he had something to search for nightly. One night he could not find it. He had trouble breathing and felt cramped as if children were lying on top of him. Crushing the air out of his lungs. He thought he was looking at things on a slant. I admired him for trying to say things he didn't know how to put into words and for the way he looked in the two tiny passport photos stuck to his door. I brought him a vase of red carnations surrounding a single white rose. They looked fake under the fluorescent light. The respirator made monstrous sounds. It made him shiver and drool. He never could keep quiet. He tossed his legs. His stomach bloated. Once he stopped resisting he became the soft innards of this groaning robot. He accepted the machine as a benevolent and life-sustaining force. And the candy stayed hidden in the over-hanging lampshade above him.

When lightning entered my body, it left a deep wound. It exited the thigh, rendering me unconscious and otherwise unharmed. I sat still on the doorstep of abstraction. He wouldn't touch anything metallic during a thunderstorm. He tore up his diaries years ago, thinking it better to have the most supple and amorphous past possible. But somehow he had kept a box of unusually shaped tokens. I took them out one by one and made an inventory. I described them. Let them edit and order a version of my life. Ten or fifteen steps on a staircase. Fingers and sometimes toes. Thirteen or fourteen cars parked along the street. I got caught in the association of mathematics with my body. A coil of rope. A lotus flower. A tadpole. A man with upraised arms. The idea of one deity gives people a sense of superiority over all those who disagree. The same song over and over. Eleven or twelve rose bushes in the garden. Beyond four, our eyes alone cannot tell us how many things there are. I left him threading beads onto wires. I was all ears.

The only sound I hear comes from circulating fans. Harsh chemicals rush through the air. My nostrils burn. In tears I pick up the scissors and snip off the hospital gown that covers him. Carefully, I tug off his boots and the latex shorts. His now icy hands once had red socks on them. He used to do bilingual puppet shows. Colored dye trickles into his underlying tissues. I pinch the plumped fingers and earlobes. The skin rebounds. He loved a well-filled bookstore. I stuff the incision in his arm with cotton balls, squirt a big glob of sealing compound on top, and sew the wound shut with a baseball stitch. He kept pestering me to make my homemade peach ice cream. It takes a long time to shave every hair from his body. I stuff cotton into his anus with practiced probing fingers. So young. So unresponsive. He said it made him feel like a woman. I rub massage crème into his face and hands. It has no smell. I stipple pinkish tones across his cheeks to raise a blush. He was never shy. I darken the eyebrows. Apply lipstick. Not-a-waitress red. More rouge on the backside of his hands. He said I was a sick fucker. I buff and paint each fingernail. Red. Red. Red. He liked it ugly and risky. All the time. I slip his favorite pair of panties on him. The black silk doesn't catch on his hairless legs. The matching bra is stuffed with cotton and the red socks. I strap it to his chest. I drape the fluffy gown over him. It's slit down the back. I push his arms through the long sleeves. The dress is loose and billowy. The color of his face. I lift his head. His thoughts about me already irretrievable fossils. I tug the raven black wig down hard over the thin pale skin that covers his skull, using some of the sealing compound to keep it in place. A pink scarf around his neck. A simple knot. I whisper in his ear. That old theory about time and unfinished people who always come back as ghosts. How they try to suck me back into the person I used to be. His eyes are still open. They look past me. Stargazing again.

one

He did, after all, have a deathbed conversion. Insight into evangelical thinking. Not always humanitarian, but useful. Dangerous visions conjured up strange old fears. Mediocre stuff filled in most of the gaps. Otherwise, the museum would become too overwhelming. He loved forbidden things. Found in the library. Without much effort. Containers of silent speech. Each one captured a steady stream. The end of my idea of love. He remained an unshakable presence. Quiet only in sleep. I took to biting my knuckles, while he aspired to give ever more precise interpretations. This severed the links in our network of hidden affinities. If you can't resist the temptation to yell in public, do so with a phone to your ear. He says his voices are witty and supportive. Only occasionally cruel. After a quick falafel. I felt like shit. The color of redwood bark on a name tag. His office was noisy. So he took a day off. He had an affliction due to the appearance of foreign images. They accompanied brash sounds. If only I could have read everything there. It was exasperating. He uncovered a whole new set of chores. Choose one and discuss. There are no connections between his extensive views. That's not a good sign. It's crucial to determine how the voices manifest themselves. Migraine headaches follow the impulse to illustrate them. Private wishes are written with children's blocks and printed on thin rectangles of handmade paper.

Sometimes, he can only think of what he will never be able to do. The problem of owning instead of renting. Someone else's right thing. Crushing a bedbug. A difficult decision. What a softy he is. Something inside him wants to hurt me. So full of things. Jokes. Bad smells. The odd use of heartlessness. The rude characterizations. References to old books. He spent so much time trying to remake them into usable structures. He hangs his inner process on them. Just like me. He's capable of dastardly behavior. Unavoidably engrossed in the details and defects. No chords. Only the sound of my head beating against the wall of a windowless and doorless cell. A twitch. A scratching of the nose. A colorless whistle. Some part of me wanting to die. The same part that's ready to kill. He has a way of making everything I do seem unimportant. But he doesn't mean it. I will have an ego. Immense. In an instant it can make me forget him. I become the citizen of this other world. The objects discussed are merely mirages born out of despair. Speak them. Or throw them away. Why do we expect gratitude from the reintroduction of other ideas into our own? What makes that so appealing? More and more. Like surprising an old friend. We're decent people here. Decent people don't give alternative histories. They let the dead vanish. There is no continuity. Not much physical evidence left. A senseless road. Marked in each example. Where one keeps slipping in the dark. Ending up on one side or the other. Out of balance. Always a peculiar and awful taste. Twisting around inside. I like it when he calls me daddy. Some of my come landed on the sheets in shapes I'd only seen in his drawings. The ones I'd helped him organize.

He invented forbidden things. Blunt. Full of anxiety. Racking up the let downs that come with these firsts. I was thinking fuck you. I wanted to eat what he perfectly arranged on the linoleum. Between his legs. He wore ripped-up fashion accessories from a boutique. Feigning indifference. His head thrown back. I thought so hard that he was no longer a possible object. He became an imaginary being. I thought he would appreciate spontaneity. I thought he would be grateful. Instead he lost his erection. Avoiding the shame of the familiar. Yes. In the middle of nowhere, everything eventually becomes landscape. Rushing by us between stops on a train. Letting go of whatever knowledge and history were once locked up in these stories. Circles within circles. Smaller and smaller. See how little room the dead require. In a world of only liquids, walls are always changing. Always hidden. The café where I write these words was a convenience store. Just weeks ago. Numerically sensitive readers will have noted how my voice has changed. Once again. They will detect a delicate mechanism operating. I refuse to be entirely absent. Unbuilding something is like being caught with our pants down. Big smiles on our faces. Still, no one is ever quite sure how we've touched each other during an encounter.

Looking too closely can be dangerous. It can ruin a positive outlook. I have to live with that. The role of pressure inside the eye suggests the structure of an organism is a system of constraints. I feel more and more distant from the objects around me. To enter the next room provides a better perspective on the one you are leaving. But often the difference between the two is negotiable after a while. He liked me for my uniqueness. He didn't know how to think clearly. And that tired me out. I brought him a banana cream pie. We ate his chicken soup. He'd put too many cloves in it. He didn't stop talking. It looks like another dense and consuming read. A high ceiling. One more offhanded remark. I snuck it in. To start the little games again. Tension is useful. Best suited for linear beings. Never remind men that their dominance is fragile. A spider interrupts the patterns of vibrations and decides whether to attack, to approach amorously, or remain hidden. I felt the delicate sound of my thoughts suddenly stretched in all directions. Like plants. They branched. Tiny painted paper partitions. Touching one another. Attaching. Then contracting. They form a bridge of infinitesimal plate-shaped crystals. They slide past each other. In the chasm that separates domains. Morning dampness and cold. Shadows fall on rich dark tones. Next to nothing. Every day warrants some kind of reportage. I had some wedges of avocado. How long does a mirror contain its own image? Only through the slow accumulation of experience comes the ability to support a constant or static load. Careful consideration of every action undermined the direction of these words. No end to the questions that arise during the hours of waiting. The end of a tiger. The end of a fern.

He traveled a long time within the wear and tear of daily life. But he began to watch the world being constructed inside him. As if he had suddenly entered someone else's little game. No longer the barefoot pilgrim on the very first page. He began to leave things out. The accuracy of spacing. The straightness of the row. The regularity of the grid. He merged things together in all kinds of odd configurations until they were lost. It became an experiment. To notice the movement from one world to another one. To break down the fluent crossings. To look harder in those in-between places. The not quite places. A fount of knowledge that broke down the dams. No longer managing the voices or trying to eradicate them. They chipped away at the obvious. Dependent on strange whims that would never dissipate completely. They violated the boundary between pain and pleasure. In the museum they took flash pictures. Nonstop. The glass partition was specially tempered so the paint wouldn't fade. Two lilies in a field of weeds. Some things are universal because they decided it was so. Exotic merchandise nuzzles and wounds you at the same time. The full impact of its charms. Watching a window that is set up. But empty. A contractual agreement for silence. To quell the discussion that defines how we see. A highly organized form of pretending. Hovering there in the background. Having lost the sense of direction once again. The location and access to information required for understanding. Gone. When is it too late to learn how something works? It's easier to live as if they don't matter. It doesn't hurt me. But I miss the attention. I don't pick up. I'd rather fall back into sleep. Slowing down. Arms and hands. Without sensation. No longer interested in architecture. Ambiguous about the destructive forces. About love. It's best when it's not an especially beautiful movement. Nor a goal-oriented gesture.

I plan in secret. The next eventful meeting. I imagine the possible scenarios. What can we make of our attentiveness? I always had trouble recognizing differences of intensity. If they weren't large enough. Any pebble in a pile. He held out his hands. I thought for the soap. He was just some ball of life. Babbling. Fingers and sometimes toes. Neither of us had enough tenderness. He whispered in my ear. How I want a drink, alcoholic of course, after the heavy lectures on quantum mechanics. A bubble bath. Leaving a messy trail. Two hands and a foot. I gave up the whole idea of preserving exactness in language. He said. If you don't follow technology, you will be deleted. What could be worse than a cold asshole? He wore a coat with dozens of tiny papers fixed to it. Each paper had words on it. Each word was replaced by the number of letters in it. Numbers written in vertical strokes. There in the empty space I created by waiting for closure. They make a tide that comes into me and back out again. It leaves dark slimy things and solid fragments of matter that I pick up and hold to feel their well-worn smoothness. A lotus flower. Another man with upraised arms. A body still afraid of geometry. It doesn't matter what I do with them. They come and go. They are perfect. Finally. Without intention.

Seamless evidence of the past. What can you do with what you've done? He said. The correct answer can't be just seen. They have to be counted. But I can't count loss and confusion. It's not like threading beads onto wires. Everyone is always dying. Dropping like flies. We use stones as a tally. But quantities are always vague. Our eyes alone don't tell us how many there are. It's beyond the limit of my natural ability to numerate. I see myself again on the doorstep of abstraction. But I have already stepped inside.

I bought a device for killing mosquitoes. It looked like a tennis racket with electrically charged strings. He was tall. Well done. Fingers like eels. A burning skull tattooed on his shaved head. A tongue of fire licking down the ridge of his spine. Calm. High-tech goatee. Lips looming large and idiotic. Slow burn. Out. Completely lunch. He told me I was a good writer. My fist pumped his ass. I'm not a writer. I just fix other people's stories. A series of snapshots capturing an aspect of this movement. Not only penetration and withdrawal. This gesture traces a large circle of awareness. Torn pieces of cardboard were stapled to his walls. He starred in thirty porn films in just two years. Oozing apple pie pessimism. An untamed jungle craving non-profit status. A dangerous ride where intentions never guarantee the actual communication of ideas. Nothing bothered him. He ate the shit out of my ass. And jerked off with it. Perfect artistry inspired by the stink. I savored the cloying odor of his gardenia-scented soap on my fingers. He entered some kind of stasis. An interim. A lightly shifting trance. We are so much more fluid than we can ever admit. I smoked one of his cigarettes. Chunks of story still tumbling down his heaving chest. The collision

45

of hideous and beautiful becomes my illusion. Translating a foreign language back into my own. I shudder in astonishment. Three days later. At the thought of my hand deep inside him. My long thumbnail slitting the tender membranes. Semi-permeable ecstasy. A ring of light bulbs in front of the images. A choice nightmare. He gave me his card. But there aren't enough layers of meaning to return to. Blurred edges. I can't rediscover how I found pleasure there. Next time. My character will stalk a cunning skein of ironies. Soft adolescent boys on skateboards that slide through the mind untouched and vanish.

I felt heat through the blankets. Him talking in his sleep. In the other language. I wanted to cry. I loved the impossibility of understanding. I whispered back. Wondering which words entered him and stuck there. Why didn't I? Push pins. Thumb tacks. Fish hooks. Single letters. I read his whole library as he slept. What governed my criminal entrances? I could always travel. Passing messages in the dark afternoons of silent movies. Repeating every day thoughts. Reformulating the projected image as a system of joints and weights. We can only guess at what lies underneath the blanket. Gibberish? More damaged than I knew. He said. He was always terrified. This struggle was his highest reason for existing. He has no sense of boundaries. That terrible tendency to alter the other person as much as possible. Beyond a cure. Politics is like someone with multiple personalities. Millions of contradicting stories buried there. Layer upon layer. Row after row. A family likeness oozes out of rotting boxes into the water supply. Embalming a corpse makes it a poison. Each stone inscribed with the same pithy text. Dominos. A sequence unearthed. A succession of states with predetermined routes. A code of raised dots. A matrix corresponding to the letters of the alphabet. A constant loudness in which the villain creates his own paradoxes. He knows manmade structures are rarely cylindrical. He loses most of his vocabulary in the dead of night. A puff of air. A square piece of ivory. The unceasing ocean waves. Their rhythm is smooth. Unbroken. Beat after beat. He lets the water come into him.

Who brings home books in the middle of a nomadic life? No more catching fish and turtles. No more catchy tunes. He can't deal with the world. It's not simple enough. We all need to stop working these useless jobs. He has a strange rapport with the problems of famous women. Never enough rehearsal time. His accent is lovely. Not resolvable. His mind stutters with every inane phrase. A generation fights his demons in their sleep. So counterproductive. So rare. This appearance of reality that cheats the senses. I can feel him moving again. That way dancers move with their bodies. The potential of all imaginable postures. Perpetual mobility. His bed has twenty little pillows on it. Where the hairs of our heads mingled. Animated conversation became increasingly private. Intimate. Frail. Like great luminous eggs. He was so far away from what I am. Yet I was drawn to his illusions. They were left on display. A single leg appeared in the trunk of his car. My perverted stranger. Born with twelve fingers. The two outer ones chopped off after his direct exposure to air. Everything extra is revealed in that shadowless light. The unexpected slides into view and is taken away. Torn from the canvas with a flat piece of metal. A misuse of power.

The wonder and the horror. A later part doesn't have to be a mirror of the earlier part. Separate the segments. Lay them side by side. Two quite different points obscured in perfect darkness. In that first breath.

What could he be writing about? We are both in each other's way. Bottling each other's essences. The quest for understanding. A struggle for power and identity. Together. Willy-nilly. Beautiful and hideous. Simultaneous. Not easily divided into equal parts. That in itself is not so awful. But I keep coming. Up out of dreaming into my bed. On the verge of awake. Falling back. The continuous motion. A white ribbon of road at night. Driving on and on. Always the same. Winding and winding. Some new buildings. Off to the side. Scenery never seen before. I brought in elements from the outside. Strawberries in cream and sugar. Buying stamps from a machine. No poetry there. No reason I can think of. And chairs everywhere. It gets harder to link all these different points in time. I have to push it all out of my head to do the writing. Until there's no center left. Not even one I can find inside myself. Numbers themselves do not mean anything. He designed the leisure time of other people. He invented the qualities of the actual moment on a keyboard. Weird stones he wore around his neck on chains. He touched them as he recounted long lists of names. Maybe that was his joke. He mumbled them to himself. Softly. Loudly. Backwards. He whispered them. Crying. What occurs in one region awakens echoes in other regions. Only the raw ideas are interesting. They show up in the longhand version. Improvements follow. The snags smooth out in a rough fabric. Typed perfectly. At the end of it all. He always says the same thing. I have no one but you.

Some pictures reach into him. How things are in the world does make a difference in his actions. But he makes up the meanings in isolation. It's something of a sport. He pretends there is only an inside. Sitting in this tight enclosed space. He develops an in-depth study of reader abuse. He's wearing a full-length waterproof bodysuit. A surgical cap and latex gloves. A clear plastic splashguard over his face. The mixture of chemicals makes a caustic vapor. A thick fog that allows him to forget the vastness of the landscape. For a few minutes. He inhales and concentrates on what's immediate in a very clear way. He is impelled to reinvent what exists beyond those pictures. Based on the few indistinct impressions that remain. Small changes lead to larger ones. He conjures up new images. Continuously. Certain rhythms are underscored as he integrates discoveries back into his viewpoint. An inexact composite is constructed and begins to infiltrate a whole new set of practices. He has become difficult for me to read. He grabbed my hand at awkward moments. I feared his gestures of affection were false. Kisses on my ear. Without letting go of my wrist. In the library he took off his shoe and ran his bare foot against my leg. I sensed oldness and decay from rows and rows of abandoned vehicles. The parking lot of a forgotten age. Lies piled up all around me as he went on improving his big misunderstanding. Something chaotic. A tumor-like mass of unregulated growth. A collection of personalities cobbled together. Lost inside these ancient word machines. Tiny models. Oblique and silky-shadowed. Becoming characters in my lack of narrative. One hopes for the best. For a plan that must be better than the one we are stuck inside. Actually. I just wanted to be alone again. Oh well. There's always some spectral residue that never gives the reader a chance to pause.

I told him old people have their own speed. A certain slower motion as they move through time. It draws something out. A giddy restlessness before sleep. The only thing we could agree on was that we didn't want to change. An illusion the size of a dinner plate. I changed more quickly than I thought humanly possible. He hung on until he was yesterday. And then tried to suck me back into the person I'd already forgotten. Was it him or me? The surfaces become so slippery. How do we lose the ability to vibrate at just the right frequency? Statues. Sitting three feet apart. Not speaking. By this time. He was his own brand. With the right markings. And tailored advertisements to match. Even the most elaborate pollination systems have a unified goal. But we were just a bunch of ideas that couldn't coalesce. A well-filled bookstore and a forest full of tiny iridescent bees. I reminded him there was really no such thing as a free sample in a widely practiced economy. He did his next somersault and I inserted my opinions into his openings. He said it made him feel like a woman. Like he had the urge to act like one. He was my escape hatch once again. It felt good. But I was oddly detached from everything. We made this exclusive arrangement. Positioning him as the bogus female. His eyes were shaped differently than mine. I hear multiple echoes of the old pictures held in place with interior monologues. In the end the toughness of our bond dissolved into debasing embarrassments. An obstacle course. Where payment was nothing more than sweetened water.

I used what I had at my disposal. I examined his room more carefully. It is here that all analogies must be attacked. As colors change they make objects acquire importance. It's a shady intimacy of exteriors and surfaces. I picked up the lacey black panties he wore under his nice suit. The smell alone implied penetration. I was distracted by the contact of my fingers with the material. Tactile impressions became an ambiguous thing. Something beyond all colors. My contemplation began to waver. Meaning giving way. Melting together. Into a wave. A piece of something caught in my throat. Hard feelings that don't subside. Covering me. In my hand I clutched the coldness spreading into his personality. A stone mausoleum or an empty bowl. Ziggurats and playing cards. Dizzying speeds and chicken soup. Various trains.

We talked science incessantly. Reinforcing each other's audacity. It was theater for me as well as pleasure. How difficult to be moving through something so big. One can never determine its shape. Without a common standard of measurement there are no relative positions. We don't have precise words or the correct number of spaces. During the period of greatest sensitivity we each see a similar shade of blue. Life loses its ongoing character and settles into a modest but sustained bourgeois contentment. I see this in every newspaper. Ice tea and hot pumpkin pie. A wad of cotton to test for touch. A safety pin to test for pain. We fell so far from unprecedented freedom. The social dimension of experience was muted. He remembered things he never knew. I collaborated with another part of myself. Both lost in the richness of variegated detail. Waiting for a shift in contrast. A flattening out. It became attractive to tell ourselves what we didn't want to know. Evolution is a tinkerer. We learn how to trace the outline of a star in the mirror. Still. There's no point in it. Only by writing can I keep alert. He said this as he sucked on the end of his pen. Travel is impossible. The backwater is drying up.

Frequent and catastrophic fires distort the sense of balance. I guess you can try too hard. Sensitive patterns are put at peril. An accumulation of keywords will not tell you what something is. A momentary glance destroys the pictures. In the oldest sense of the phrase. Interpret everything as you wish. He defrosted the freezer. Obsessed with remote biographical anecdotes. Always searching out the hidden structures of literature. It's understandable. He looks for a place where he cannot be reached. Where he can grasp newness in order to measure it. Averting the old panic. Once there. He remembered the lights of the car. Moving around and around in the same spiraling loop. More traffic noises. Falling off the edge of the circle. Oblivion can be stressful. He lost whole paragraphs while counting empty chairs. Truckloads of venom. Another's thoughts. A mere creature of my mind. A fragile shadow. Can he thrive under this florescent light? I make him disappear as I look for ways to make him say things he never could before.

When I lie on my back so much of the old me returns. Confused. Demanding. Unrepentant. Irrational. Pig-headed. He was suspicious of the calm. It's not that hard to be a murderer. At first anyway. I could have done it. If things had happened differently. I get so tired of waiting for people to notice. Patriotism is exasperating on television. I watched it paralyze a country. Little black and white webs of intrigue twisted around inside me. He had the advantage of other experiments. Pages of results. The main character described a terrible situation. As a child, his parents forced a personality on him. As an adult, he forced it on everyone else. His room had only one window. One chair. One box of tissues. How hard it is to represent therapy accurately. Despite appearances. Rigidly drawn lines cease to be simple. He said I should feel free to ask questions. He is after all my friend. He had thrown out that old sofa. I said I liked it. And what we'd done on it. He said I shouldn't be satisfied with marginal illumination. You have to swim in it. Spend time in it. Tea cups and guide books. Consider it a box. Just like everyone else. It makes everything transparent. I said I moved through worlds to see what response I would get. He said that's not really a story. What does it mean? I can't inhabit certain thoughts. I hate being the one who has to wait. Retracing movements just leaves another pathway back. Dot. Dot. Dot. Who's counting? I developed a resistance to his progressively insistent probing. He couldn't resist the impulse to search. A night nurse looking for hidden candy. I don't trust perfect solutions. He said taking risks is important in order to make advances. I recalled the last moving scene. The distinct impression of doubling. When he shook my hand he looked at the floor.

Now. I spread two fingers apart and point to my eyes. I'm standing on the edge. Not pulled in. Never staying in the center. The core is a void. A sticky abyss. Home is the most uncomfortable place to be. Airless. I am a shadow. A separate movement. His diversion. A back-talking bird whose speech speaks only of itself. I make meaning out of certain lines. But only when they intersect in groups. A wonderful display. Individual pages made of light. Viewable from either side. I gaze at them for a few seconds at a time. Avoiding the damage that comes from continual exposure. Voices rise on top of each other. Most words are garbled. And most worlds. It looks like chaos. His books are overdue. He wrote them because he wanted to have a good laugh at himself in the future. His problem was never holding back. He continued despite the urge to describe everything in a stable and on-going clarity. He wanted a world where the endings came as a series of astonishing revelations. Where thought and thing are one. He used to hunt through catalogs. Trying to find the right order numbers. An unexpected consequence was the blurring of distinction between text and images. To this day he has trouble locating where writing leaves off and matter begins. He's suspicious of television screens. It's having a brain full of someone else's heirlooms. I'm learning to relish his blind spots. He fosters an obsession with encryption and gave up an addiction to wishful thinking. He was tired of building the great wall. Instead. I began to bring it down. Stone by stone. No more despair about being misunderstood. A shift of emphasis from letters to the envelopes that hold them. Notice the interplay of these words and the surfaces of objects. Shining moments. Funny beliefs. Silence stretches out between me and the world of absolute answers to everything. I wish I could invent a way to talk about what's hidden on the other side. The place where the holes in my language end up.

Both of us wrote by hand. Side by side. Our handwritings almost identical. His was differently sloped. Which one is the remake? Mine had a fucked-up soundtrack. He thought the end had to be the best part. I wasn't so sure. I wanted the voices to run on and on until they found something no individual voice knew was there. I couldn't stop ideas as they entered. I made room for them. I was not afraid of what poked out between the halves of the unzipped zipper. He was frustrated when I put my hand there and felt around. But he didn't stay nervous for long. The tension subsided. Old patterns of longing gave way. The light from a full moon is reflected starlight. We played hide and seek in the dark fortress of identity. Acts of secret chemistry. A little ruthless. The paths of the others were always more compelling. Today's entry is full of lies. Even fragments have a sense of hierarchy. I picture us as two selfish snowmen. Believing we're impervious to the hot summer rain. A successful life experiment. Malady free. Archeologists of buried selves intersecting. Layers upon layers. The melancholy logic of contradictory impulses. Insight into the little shadows that go in and out. I stayed up several nights in a row. Learning the lines and rehearsing them in his room. I stole his books. I kept changing scenes. I thought it possible to replace fantasy. I severed the arms of our cartoon likenesses. I put trouble back in paradise. Soon he bore the marks of prolonged neglect. His text was an illegible scrawl on my machine. A dim fire undermined by the rivers of ink from my fountain pen. He used to suck the end of it.

When I'm with someone, I struggle to find what I am. Sometimes lightning goes through the body and leaves a deep wound. In a refrigerated room behind the chapel, there is the sound from the circulating fans. He grabs the edge of the plastic bag and pulls me from the gurney onto a metal table. Taking care not to bump my nude body. A pink lifelike tinge returns to my ashen skin as colored dye trickles into the underlying tissue. He pinches my fingertips and earlobes. He fills my mouth with putty and with a small-gauge needle injects tissue builder along the outer edges of both lips. He pushes them into a gentle upward curve and glues them permanently shut. In the background the same song plays over and over again. By now, he's torn up my diaries and burned them. He carefully makes up my face. Matching the look of the photograph he's placed beside me on the table. He follows the makeup with light rouge. White baby powder is dusted on top of that. Eyebrows are darkened and lipstick applied with a fine brush. My hair is brushed back and set with a hardening gel. He opens the wooden box I carried around for years and puts each object on the table by my head. He selects one and wraps it in a ball of cotton. He cups my hands around it, left over right, and rests them in my lap. He gently tilts my head a little to the side and whispers in my ear. Don't fight it. Give in to it. Fix your mind on this one white flower. Empty yourself of every other thought. Follow the motion of water. Swirling around. Steady. Deep. Dark. Strange how the light is reflected on the waves. Little specks that move into you. Let them come into you. The caressing waters closing over you. Tugging you down. Down. Down.

JA, MEHR: LA MER

Quoting gets on my nerves. But we are sequestered in a world that is constantly quoting, in a constant quotation that is the world…

Thomas Bernhard —*Gargoyles*

…every piece you put in fits, and then when you finish it, you see that it's not the picture. Then you do another version and it's not the picture. Finally you realize you are not going to get a picture.

Morton Feldman —*Give My Regards to Eighth Street*

…perhaps it's the sea that never leaves them alone, that's always there making a noise…

Marguerite Duras —*Blue Eyes. Black Hair*

I've arrived in the middle of something. My hands are numb. I can't completely relax and enjoy chewing. I want it to be more than it is. And less pain in places I can't quite locate. It keeps coming apart and I'm getting used to it. That's a good sign. I'm not even sure when it started. We made catfish. It was better the second time. A big sore on his lower lip. It's been a struggle to get things set up. They told me I'm supposed to have special gifts. A silk robe for my little dinosaur. But mainly it's positive obsession and persistence. I hurt people's feelings. It's a way to scare people into thinking. The blonde waiter told us to take our hats off. It happens in cathedrals, too. There are a lot of ways to look back, you know. To clarify things in the immediate vicinity. I no longer have a point of reference for remote objects. They've already gone missing. Maybe I should see a shrink. Learning to blame others and yourself and making that a form of control. Letting it all go isn't an option. There isn't a whole world. There's only the idea of one. Something has changed the shape of the walls. Oh no. Another story about a man in a box for long periods of time. Something else is there. Sounds are taking the place of his body. But who put him in the box? Twigs. Paper. String. A bit of down. Who made him a landscape? Who drew those clumsy pictures on the outside? Maybe there's more than one existence in the space and time a body occupies. I voted for no fault insurance. It feels like everybody trying to recapture the pages lost in an erratic mechanism. The songs blur together. He bought his gold dragon. I thought it was gross, but the color looks good on his skin. When he moves, the halogen spots that shine on the metal make little rays of light. They look as if they are shooting out of his solar plexus. Most are easier to recognize in flight. He needs to start thinking about his future. He staples white cardboard rectangles to the walls next to fuzzy panoramas from a hundred years ago. Foreign cities he can't identify. But he's familiar with the skin that covers every building. Every street. Pores full of grit and dirty water. Waiting for the last grain to fall through the neck of the hourglass. At night I'm the only one left alive. I compare the new ones to the original until I can't tell which one is which. Red light bulbs in a circle behind transparent images. It's a mistake for sure. I can't swallow. The most recent chapters too valuable to give up. Walking out without paying the bill.

My heart pounding. Running through a casino. Someone guards a slot machine for a friend. A voice like a cartoon mouse. White-rumped. Such a hoot. Zoom. Boom. Zoom. Three bean sonata queen. Pink lemonade. In a hammock. Tied to a tree. Gently rocking. Eyes on the barbed wire that lines the fence. Back in ten minutes. Back and forth. My thoughts clipped off and overthrown. The fragile moments. Bent out of shape. Incompatible with my present state. Why don't I say anything? I want your number. Yes. The little games with listening and numbers. Counting biscuits. But I can't do it. I have no idea what to do next. This should be a good thing. I woke up bothered one morning. In the back of a house. In the backyard. The letters of his name on a chain around his neck. Broken toys everywhere. We played cards for money. He had affection for competitive get-togethers. I can't get the work done that way. I have to move. I have to find the next place. Somewhere they won't look. It's going to be a good weekend. Time is a luxury. The computer is an oven that cooks my brains. Barefoot and pregnant with words. I keep my eye on the shelf. In a kitchen. Under the pots or in the broom closet. You have to start somewhere. A job steals you. Certain music is the perfect accompaniment for writing. For biting off a finger. He beats his foster kids that way. Would it help to turn him in? I doubt it. Bitchy and frustrated. A hundred dollars every visit. Start without me. Please. Redefine the reasons. I don't believe in maturity. I'm flexible. Pats on the back. Down and dirty. I'm performing so differently. It's great to see the city from above. Landmarks take time to establish. The marble and cement boxes become redundant. They send me two copies. Strange paper containers that fix my words between all the others. I like it when everybody talks at once. Yes, but you're supposed to be talking about intimacy. Well, he can barely separate pornography and the sex we have together. Is it time to re-arrange values into a new hierarchy? Uh no, keep it light and fluffy. I don't like frugal fucking. I just sent a long letter about death and creativity to him. I can't seem to stop the ideas from coming. Whose? Something to do with corpses. Even when I'm exhausted. Their lack of identity makes them me. I have access to so much information that I find myself holding back after awhile. It's not always good to share. We've forgotten that there is a special air around new forms. I can't stop being encyclopedic. I need subtitles. I need to be alone more often. Watching movies in the dark. Life never gets removed from ideas anymore. But whose are they? I can't be upset with him for that. He just wants to be with me. To have fun. If we didn't have numbers we wouldn't have to keep track. They are made out of metal. They have white, orange, or red reflectors on them. Usually three or four of them. Sometimes words and numbers. It depends on which state you're in at the time. It can take a lifetime to compile. I see the earliest moments of my childhood stretched thin like a membrane made of saltwater taffy. He's poking holes in it while it folds into itself on metal rods. The tiled floor was flooded. The odor of moldy towels. The lights didn't work. We kept falling into the crater between us in the mattress and waking each other up. The sight of whipped cream out of a can made me retch. One hundred and four. Fever in the desert. A motel of needles. The smile of an only survivor. There's always this struggle to change the other person. His mind smelled homeless. I could feel him standing inside a much older man. It's just a bigger warehouse. That intimidating

64

part of genealogy. So eager to spill the beans. To exclude everything that is not itself. The skin under my nose is infected from blowing it on paper towels. That's all I had at the time. Hot tea and more bed. I am too weak to write. But it was written all over his face long ago. It could be another stunning first effort. No. It's a celebration. It reveals a great deal. It promises to be a terrific read. It's the past always set in the future. It extrapolates things and reshapes them with technological innovation. It validates the old ones and hardly anyone notices. It suggests that all the ordeals haven't provided any answers. Just better questions. But it's vague enough that it doesn't have to read that way. Edges need slightly different treatments. A kind of world-weariness settles around them. Hey, he's feeding big nuts to mangy little squirrels. There were signs on the trees instructing people to step on the man that was lying in the grass. Only women were walking on him. Dogwoods in bloom. An undisturbed pool with orange and white carp. More stones than flowers. Colors only found in nature. I prefer the preparations from the leaves. A tincture of calm whispers. Hidden messages. He assured me that if the rocks in a garden are not monstrous, the scholars get bored. The printer went wacky. Black ink all over my hospital whites. An eight-letter word on a triple-word square. No one seems upset by it. Seventy-seven points. Unusual rules about family interaction. Addicted to junk. Piles of it all around the desk. I stayed late to correct another manuscript. While he painted the shelves black. A couple of pesky preening buzzards. Half-naked boys and stuffed animals. It's a zoo out there. Spoons on the floor. Four of a kind. Objects can be overlapped to create the illusion of depth. It only costs fifty cents. Shaved chests and new tattoos.

History is hard enough to get rid of. It still sucks my fingers. I must fabricate horizontal bonds as well as vertical. A constant source of intellectual input. A scavenger feeding on carcasses. What a nomad. I don't have to wait for him to call me. But the searching process is not always attractive. He fills in an irregular panel with a darker tone. Why do I care so much for this idea of preservation? It's closer to the bedroom. The soft white oval patches below their golden eyes. They take more than the piece of bread I offer. I refuse to sit around waiting for some half-assed version of the wilder days. I want to get somewhere I've never been. It's never an accurate recreation. Never. Replacing him is a difficult task. I crave time. We would just sit around the house and talk. It can take years to make a real transition. There isn't a proper sequence of doors. At what point does a pattern become a pattern? I was on the verge of tears as their ideas gradually worked their way into what I thought were mine. Withered flowers are cast into the oven as fuel. The mere husks of wisdom. Scarlet on snow white. Violet on flesh. Settling for a life of crime. Cuckoos laying eggs in other birds' nests. No air conditioning. Just a magnifying glass. They say the world is round and doesn't have small corners. Why question geometry? Yesterday was better. For what? Some photographer is always taking pictures. Some conversations we have too late. I guess that's typical. A pair of coils mounted at fixed angles. Horny. A bit spaced out, but very nice. Dirty water still flows downhill. A particularly eloquent passage. A tendency towards secrecy. Rape can be an enveloping as well as a penetration. Please don't let the past decide for you. Flimsy evidence on the outskirts of sacrilege. I can get nasty after a while. All the while. Wanting something back. Maybe later.

Find your own way. Navigate the current mess. I just wanted to be alone, damn it. To make a talking diary. To get a little more precise. Something followed by a hundred zeroes. A jumble of emotions. Thinking in terms of oppressor and oppressed. It makes no difference if I test an invention in my mind or with an actual model. He was dozing on the subway. Someone tried to grab the gold chain with his dragon hanging from it. The thief's fingernail sliced the skin under his chin. He said I would never find anyone that thinks like I do. He watched me drop little squares of blank paper into dishes filled with liquid. Each one dried into a different shape. There is a big gap between us now. He loves the smell of cooking oil. Everything has to be fried. To the untrained eye stepping-stones appear thin, but usually they are not. I can hear the sizzling of breaded pork chops on an iron griddle a block away. There are times when the sounds of the city have the effect of spoken words. I have learned to resolve them back from their accidental combinations into original components. Only then can I drift off to sleep. I draw diagrams in the night sand. In the ancient light from stars. Each one a splintered descending figure. Those painters made a terrible mess on the floor. It had charm and potential. I am a spotlight playing over an existing landscape. Not a rest in any part. I chose only trees that grow on wild hillsides. None with strong scents. Some buds of self-pollinating plants never open. A chain of solos. Bumper to bumper. The movements are so sudden, but nobody gets anywhere. I'm glad to be free of television. It's completely thankless. It made me a target for arrows. The voices can be heard long after the broadcast is complete. A little adventure would be good, though. Followed by a less obvious one. A festival. Everything shaped like electric guitars. Rude kids kept taking our triangle. No idea about tact. Who's keeping score? Eccentric words won't save us. The blank tiles can be any letter at all. Elaborate justifications about now. Is it easier to believe that everything is already complete inside us? Well, he always cries when he hears that song. And then he puts it on when people come over. In order to sleep we have to lie in the shadows of simple explanations. Listening to trite sermons. Insulting to the ears. Pigeonholes create order. Possession of a penis permits tricks that would otherwise be impossible. Or so they thought. Hanging all over each other in the front row. Scrupulous without being prickly. Turning death into a generic two-edged sword. That's his version of the blues. Health benefits. Dental plan. Full-fledged flag-waving. Paid vacation days. Things that don't take up any space. Not kept in that tiny wooden box I've been carrying around for years. With both hands I clutch at the persistent void. But I refuse to look through it. It's not a mirror. It never was. Reading magazines all day. Over and over again. Imagining the next shape instead of making this one work. Complexion rerouted into complexity. Which world interprets the other one? Negotiable differences. Revisited as a corny movie. He could sit motionless for hours in the afternoon as everything circled around him in a frenzy. It could be seen as an attempt to let the old ones come into him. He was caught in the rain. Without the wet. An anesthesia that let them come and go without him noticing. Find a way to use the research, but don't let it get in the way. Working out problems in the foreground. Nobody knows what to do with a background. Unending war and genocide. Noughts and crosses. The artists are not hungry enough these days. One of them drinks turpentine.

He appears to be a nice guy. Reads books. Likes to travel. A real crowd pleaser at heart. A slight headache. He lets a scone sprinkled with cinnamon and granulated sugar get stale before he eats it. A huge tiger tattooed on his back disappears under his shorts and continues down one leg. I'm leaving something out. All the time. I don't know what it is. There will always be holes that won't ever be filled. Every retelling brimming with spinsters. While I seek to entertain strangers. Thoughts like crystals. Quite an undertaking. They look for things to slow me down. Way down. They're so damn moody. They call this a battered condition. I wanted to buy sneakers. The kind with air in the soles. Rubber comic books for feet. Walking optimistic hard-ons under our telephones. Like dogs. He wants more realism and grunge. Ridiculous things about foreigners. Stuck under a covered sidewalk in the monsoon. Heavy drops splattered everywhere. Another mess left by the painters. At least some of it ended up on the walls. They come back again and again with love on their hands. Clean surfaces look better when the sun shines on them. Through dirty windows. This time, it's not the glass that's stained. Most never learn that everything important comes from the outside. Knocks the wind right out of me. A sneeze of words landing on freshly pressed paper. The patterns are reminiscent of incomprehensible formulas. More bookstores. A series of events. Sensible lips. What makes it tick? The gears of motivation. Thinking against expectation. A frightening idea for some. To stop before it's full. It gets harder and harder to start over. He maintains a certain remove, but stays in the realm of the personal. An emphasis on burial. This city does that to you. After a long time there is evidence of unspoken things. He says goodbye in silence.

Calculating avoidance. Desires diverging. A laminated graph that reveals the intriguing qualities of this remarkable curve. There are nice sentences that bend upward. Yet they hide their feelings. A room without a view. Somewhere along the plane of intersection between two adjoining spheres. I don't know where to put the camera. Duck. With oranges. It's up to me to collect myself. I wonder if I have the strength. To fail. To resurrect effective templates. Too hard to dwell on this now. There's more work to do. In the short term. Prettier postcards. Everything in flux. I bit my tongue. A sadness. A single harmony hovers in the cool air. What did he look like? The camera is always moving. Just a little bit. Even the audience has to crane their necks to see everything. A few grab whatever can be taken. His skin was the color of redwood bark. A fickle god. Swords and knives can be extremely seductive. Perfect madrigals. The bus ride back was a bit annoying. The unparalleled brutality left me dazed. I don't remember leaving the cinema. Maybe we never do. An attraction to strange tessellations. Not found in finer bathrooms. It gets under my skin and stays there. The violence. Put it into something else. Spinning cages. Let it be invisible. The way water smoothes pebbles over a long period. Lapsing so easily into loneliness. Make something out of all that thinking. Sounds like a job. Looking for permission to live. Ah, the candor of an arbitrary squiggle. I like wisps, too. Don't you? When nothing exceptional happens. It feeds the milquetoast journalism of the moment. More insulting in retrospect. Looking back over the rolling hills. Traces of camaraderie. A limited number of faces. The most favored rocks are old and weathered. Spirits hide beneath them and scurry away when uncovered. The dry waterfall waits for the storm. In the mood to share. Flea market. Vague ideas. I polish well-worn mirrors. Tomorrow is a half-day. A box to put things in. Tick tack toe. Something comes out ahead. They're all moving at different rates. An element of fantasy about what they do. I went back to the library for some area. Wanting more extensive notes. Interior adventures in real estate. So pliable. I poked holes in him. He was furious and wouldn't look at my face. My eyes. Colored dirt. A floating focus. I made such complicated rhythms out of simple modules. Loading boxes into a truck. A phantom limb. He might come back. The spelling of a word is still holy to some. Under a big light. This pushed it right up front. Couldn't sleep at all. Nostalgia for the old black and white ones. Plans for dismemberment. Degraded images at midnight. Harboring hope. That's not what he had in mind. A detail from an unending design. Such fabrics are a favorite of moths. The torture of having a feeling you can't afford to have. He liked to watch things die. Night things that flutter around porch lights. Something you don't want to know. A border of rosettes on a darker background. A hint of gold in the soft flesh of the petals. Fading into further detachment. Bring in people from the outside. The old forms are beaten into position. I read them over and over again. Hoping to avoid the same traps. I can't hate him for his confusion. I can only move away from it. Respond sooner with reason. After arranging an enormous body of facts. With respect to animals. Grazing the ear of a gazelle. The fluid linking strokes of the letters. Electricity that accumulates at various points on the skin. I have to get away from the ruins of foreign cities. When do I come to the end of an idea? He's become wary of bargains and the first few steps into new circumstances. Slices of smoked ham cut like tissue paper. Degrees of stasis. Hushed. Muted colors. Everything is a found object. Especially trousers. Comfort food. Watches with dials. The rain came in sprinkles and drove the people back into the museum. A security guard shook his keys at me. I started to wander. This did not lead to a decline in standards. Some images are the result of a reflex action of the brain. A retina under great excitation. Loose threads on the reverse have to be trimmed so both sides appear equally finished. He was predicting how the clouds would look in five minutes while some kids stole his luggage. Making your own doesn't always save money. I make do with my old rags. Fixing the places I want to go in my mind. A transom turned into a coffee table. A handful. Trying to open a map in the wind. When I spread it out on the floor at home, the cat always sits on the outskirts. Facing southwest. I plan our next meeting in secret. Drawn in various poses. There are openings for umbrella-leafed quills. Fingers trace the star-shaped core. The silver is pierced to allow incense to escape. I will move through thousands of pieces. He watched me take all the money out of his wallet. Not enough tenderness. He held out his hands. I gave him back two dollars. It was not egg on his face. Unorthodox theories. Coarse and unsigned. With crudely embroidered flower motifs. He held out his hands again and gazed into his polished thumbnails. A draining comes with it. No matter how nice you want to be. Brittle pages melted into his body and revived him completely. Maps make nice companions for settling into old age, but do not always offer sound advice. Late in the afternoon there are blood tests. My chest is congested. I bought a copper lamp and lit a candle inside it. Slept in his bed for a week without him. Intersecting diamonds of shadow and light. He wore orange pants with fish swimming all over them. A silken fringe. Walking by the window a second time. We met in the vestibule. Exposing our crooked wares. Flasks with sturdy rounded bodies. Swelling at the top of the necks. An arabesque coming out of two overlaying designs. The tip of my index finger. Translucent splatter on birch wood. Smeared with rubber soles. Once upon a time. It could be breakfast. Every day. A store full of masks. The tooth from a grackle's palate. Elevators moving in opposite directions. Rejuvenating excursions. History tries to catch up. Some kid naked on the couch. Showing us his ass. Buttercup. Snuggled between cushions. We imagine curious sequences. Uncertain curves dominate the moment. A compact scroll. With stretched and bent letters. Verses recited over the shoulder bones of an ox. The gallery was stifling. We went back out into the rain. He knew the artist. Over drinks. Tiny filaments drifting in tangles. Wrapping around whatever's handy. Full of himself. He plopped face down on the bed. Early civilizations wrestled in his head. Oiled beasts in single file. Tarred and feathered. Their handprints on his trapezoidal planks. The abundant seeds of a new language. I played quirky tunes on the jukebox. Thick amber glaze. Fat gemstones hung there. With serpentine fragments. Sharp and slippery on knotted cords. Too lazy to use coupons. Vegetarian lunchbox. Some beer. Movies and bed. He relaxed so I could see the hurt in him. Skirting leftover affection. If the edges are frayed. Trim them. Another beer. The next picture depicts the cumulative effect. Smoothed-over cloud. I gave him a back rub. When do thoughts stand still? It's chilly in there. Not mindless. Just some unknown mix. He had no interest in the future. If it doesn't exist yet it doesn't make sense. Looking back from event to event. The rhythm just changes. Another genre emptied of its terror. The landscape is rendered harmless again. I wanted appalling moments. Something amateurish and homely. The best humor lies somewhere in our incompatibility. The new asymmetrical temple. To house these images. His watch stopped. Sixth row center. Tired baby. A confusion of the senses. He spilled his beer on me and gave me the first fifty pages of a novel. Slept until noon. Hung over geysers. Bad breath kisses. More gruesome cartoons. Misunderstood fantasies. How sad the music is from this part of the world. The ice cream trucks go back and forth all day. Perky lament in tinsel. The spiraling chat whistles. Drooping downwards in major. The inevitable weight. Yellow-breasted. Centuries of resignation. Is it always a crime to appeal to the sensitivities of the enchanted spectator? For some, tomorrow is always the last day. They get strangely excited about nothing at all really. Happy endings. New clothes and some furniture. The next thing I know he's curled up on the bathroom floor. Nude and dizzy. His austerity was moderated by elegant undulations. A puddle of walnut fudge. Molten for an instant on the white tiles. Just before it slips into the dark chasm. Solidified. It's dangerous to travel there. He grabs my hand when I stop thinking about him. Kisses in the music store. I need a better grip on the timeline. Texts. Heroics. Gods. Cities. The decline of an era. The end of a ruling people. Shovelers in the short dense grasses. I could see blood vessels in my eyes. The doctor touched my leg as I struggled to read the tiny letters. Which is better? One or two? There's frost on the windows. Sometimes paired. No heat from the radiators. He always gets my machine and leaves me progressively smaller stories. Hot tea with milk in a transparent mug. This tendency to cling to single ideals. Strength through narrowing. Sunken rectangles in the ceiling. Sickened by tunnel vision. I try to fight certain qualities. I find them at snowmelt. They creep down slope with the sudden movement of loose stones. The internal avalanche in slow motion. This is one of the best things about living alone. I never have to change for anyone else. I can change into something from the inside. Winning at solitaire. Losing one illusion for the sake of another. In between them I lose the domination of the main character. Two loads of laundry. Two bags of groceries. Naps. A mouse runs into a hole in the wall I didn't know was there. He used to sit backwards in that chair. Parroting my scribbles. He accused me of asking children for content. Do you believe what your shirt says? All the time? When are thoughts about pictures more important than the pictures? The students ask questions like this. I collect scads of them and rearrange them. I change them into something from another time. The unfocussed landscape. Colored powder in a tin. How rare invention really is. To lose sight of the recipe. Caught in a cloudburst. Neighbors swept away by the deluge. Showing slides of old pyramids. Wearing the same old jeans. Sad creatures lost in a web of intrigue. Some observers don't live to tell the tale. The passionate kaleidoscope of crystal gazing. What he wanted most stayed in a sphere of glass. We pay to keep things out of reach. Semi-detached. Scraping off the scabs of others. Dark areas create depth on a finished surface. Blunt and full of typos. Humor trickles through it. Flustered by a crying child. Imposing odd punishments on the innocent. A national pastime. He chose a strange method of protecting what provides flavor and bright blooms. Vulnerable to unexpected blasts of arctic air. I spit in his mouth. Honking horns and firecrackers set off a game of chance. What we aren't supposed to like makes empty spaces beautiful. He looks confident until the uniform comes off in my hands. He finds absence only through the use of indirect language. Seduced by the magic of what is arbitrary. Every night. Raunchy weather for weeks. He stays in the place where events move from the immediate future and attach themselves to the past. Eyeing a mirror made of steel during the waxing of the moon. He caught himself looking at what he was making. And became the hostage of time. A single black dot in the center of a white circle. We called it playacting. Great birds made of folded paper. Plump. With bleached hair. Pale green eyes set in varnished oak wood. The afterglow of lust. Leftover curry. Dormant craters. The second time around. The implications of every detail are allowed to speak for themselves. I don't share the same enthusiasm for operating machines. After a certain stage people applaud the war in private. Daunting offences gouge soft flesh. The perils of picking blackberries. More male things. Monotheistic rain. He goes back and forth. Reading at home to make a museum of the mind. I look for the artificial in nature. Do ducks have family values? Pay close attention to quacks and flukes. They all end up on the subway. I used to translate their songs. Strange twists in every melody. Careful rebuilding follows the most disastrous fires. He never admits his malicious intentions. Proud. Cautious. Withholding evidence. Tricky ways to invade reality from underneath. Forgetting what slowly seeps back down into the earth. I thought it was part of his costume at first. But his two front teeth were knocked out. What had come into contact with his face? A foregone conclusion? His business is to turn away from subterfuge. Fieldstones hefted into place by hand to make a rough square. Enclosing a plot of grass. These structures distract the populace. Formal curses. Moss littered with tiny scarlet beads. Caravans of soiled words fallen off their strings. I wanted a rematch. He hates to lose. But I've learned how. He drifts through a preset system of formulating questions. I borrowed a microphone. Unraveling parts of my past that wake up wrapped around each other. Some seeds pass through the body intact. I no longer take photographs that try to eliminate reflections. He threw a phone through the window. It concealed one awkward situation with another. Layers of investment. We wait to move beyond chemistry. He likes my hand the most. I leave greasy prints on glass. He told me not to be afraid of imitation. Of using past skills. My personality will seep through. I fucked him into a jelly of compliments. The magic lies in the tempting gap between what the shapes mean and what they are made of. How convenient. Make sure the condom doesn't break. I've become someone who doesn't quite exist yet. I can't stop. I'm just not geared for beginners. He gushed girlish giggles. But I've no problems holding back. I consider every action and reaction. He becomes a tarot of pheromones. Sharing a love of noxious serpents. Yes, he studied toxins and milked snakes for a living. He took his time feeling the bones inside the flesh of my fingers. Winter light fell through a copula. Slender beams pierced the beveled display cases and faded the dusty portraits of dead men. Tiny blades gleamed. Washed clean of the blood they were designed to release from opening veins. Porcelain bowls with blue cornflowers. Human remains arranged on plain white shelves and covered with an indestructible plastic sheet. The same plastic that covers his mattresses. We both end up fixed in each other's frames. Desire surrounded by a sterile field. Perpetual fuck buddies. Let's go bowling afterwards. Scorecards leave men superstitious. A history of scissors in a chest of closed drawers. Labeled in his best handwriting on small cards. Edges curling. Water damaged. Whole religions can't imagine why we fuck one after the other. Quite a scenario. Hurt me now and spare me later. Spoil my rod and find the child I will never leave behind. Such a bright reasonable approach to things. I taped over his songs. Young men are wounded in the head every day. The rest peep around corners at them. It's nearly impossible to think of glass as a liquid. Beliefs have these wonderful moments. Mistletoe is a parasite. He has trouble when I can't make definitions exact. Doing the right thing is always important. Stocks or bonds. With difficulty. I watch age take its toll. Touching on the big issues. The larger canvas is rarely abandoned in favor of the old rough sketches. He always starts over when he gets comfortable. Amputation is a bit extreme though. Imagine a spectator in place of a painting. He gazes down at the limb he is soon to lose. He puts his own finger through the hole and it passes through bone. A thin vapor and the scent of lilac fill the emptiness. The wainscoting is dark with dirt. The white stone tiles are spattered with his blood. Moths flutter nearby. There is not much of a future in formaldehyde. All his doors are blistered by fire. Someone always wants to blame the homeless. And at this point I don't know what would interest him. Even architecture has lost its splendor. He strives to build these final moments on uncertainly. And then a bag of flour. Set loose in the sea. Salty and immense. Life crawled out of it. Not bread. We somehow became a menacing presence in the world. The number of beneficial spirits dwindled. Frantic circles and the burying of wax images. Authors embed all manner of spells in their stories. Told in firelight. Empires forget how to listen. They become concerned over the tone of muscles. I could never see a dialog take place in him. One part doesn't speak to another. Shortcomings? Failures? Do you really want me to go into all this stuff? At dinner he didn't realize the girls sitting at the next table were boys. Fried bananas rolled in butter and honey. That movie is never as good as I think it is. My own dream sequences were cornier. Some things are better left to their secret places. So let's just talk sensibly. Easy thoughts. Lugging groceries. Coasting downhill. We really need a new strip mall next to the other one. Devout shopping for corporeal envelopes. We never know exactly where we are. Floating in apocalyptic haze. Three-eyed figures mounting their consorts on a magic carpet. I gorged myself on chance essays and propaganda. He listened to prophets and old church people. Toying with faggots and fetters. Developing a strict two-dimensional quality. In the background I worked with systems of angularity. Rhomboidal scrolls overlap and alternate like bell tones ringing in the tower. A narrow border will not disrupt the effect of the overall design. It gives the impression of a garden in full bloom. Bird's eye views. The veins of dried leaves once connected certain words between these pages. I want to protect him and at the same time push him over a cliff. Threatening him to be reasonable is not reasonable. I slaughtered him again and again as we played with letters. He has an emotional vocabulary. A hundred pages of discarded clothes. A quarrel better inserted into the ancient past. Disobedient sons. Sore-assed and sick the whole time. Holding each other with wet hands and closed eyes. Fingers speak across desert flesh. At the slightest pressure new leaves sprout and grow like fingernails. Our quiet is a ruse. Chaos will not hold still. We clutch tighter as we are hit with the vegetable equivalent of exploding pebble dash. Oh, it's just the alarm clock. I will never be in that exact position again. Do I write about things to remember them or forget them? Absolutely. It's become a silly sort of barrier. He really is a conniving little bitch. Yearns to be a recurring stereotype. I can't spend the whole day wracking my brain for birthday thrills. I don't have money for hotels. Dinner and theater. I don't want to give him objects. The difference between complexity and complication. Slow comfortable screw. Neither bang nor whimper. Maybe eradicating superstitious ideas. A jagged red line divides the map in two. Animal heads on one side. Human on the other. Smaller octagons follow each other into rectangular fields where rows of potted orange trees have become waxy green spheres. For a long time there were only words. Successive editions had fewer and fewer until the day only pictures were collected in albums. A couple of schoolgirls high on soap. Talking about triangles. An exercise in obliteration. The difference between men and boys. Dozing in each other's dreams. Gobbledygook. At that point it ceases to be glue. He speculated on how long it would remain hot. Certain unripe mangoes are deadly. I tend to think people should get away with things. He likes words for what is invisible. It was written all over him in a language only I could understand. His accompanying gestures reminded me of brushstrokes. The story waits for its moment. It gestates until unavoidable. I become its hostage. Marvel and persist. Surrounded by arches and borders. Beginning and end points overlap. Floating on the surface of silence. Tiny bubbles of air. Glimpses of motion frozen into structure. Two folded squares of paper. Fork in the road. One says go. One says stay. I sit for hours on that old wooden chair. Wanting everything. More chances. Dervish on a shelf. Things create effects by being there. I spit in his face and licked it off. He knew we needed a better last moment. Regret. Relief. All of the stones except one seem to be flowing from left to right. The light on them is always changing. Dragging a steel wool pad through your glaze. Crisscross. Wear goggles to shield your eyes. Latex gloves to protect your delicate hands. A mask guards against fumes. Throw wet rags soaked in turpentine on the fire. The future consists of harder materials. Exchanging needles for bolts. Trading buttons for tender blows. Hints of hesitation for seventeen days. I slowly return to myself. Uneasy and tired on the sidewalk. Break your mother's back. Drunk and chock full of nuts. Unexpected cookies crumble. But I'll never be the oldest troll at the end of the bar. Transparent flings. Mean-mouthed clowns. Shallow root systems. Swollen fickles. Thirsty ephemerals. Sweet juicy figs. Ready to enhance a seed disperser's lunch. A thousand a month to live on. Incremental bail. The jail rots inside me. Windows high on the wall. White picket fence. He sticks it through a gap between the slats. Recognized me from the old days. Pretty large doses. The postman seldom brings closure. Spectral delivery. Bubbled and rapt. Duct tape leaves that white stuff that won't wash off. Mistaken for salve. The beads of hot metal fly. Hollow teardrop ornaments hung on a background of pierced humps. Pulverized cobalt once used to imitate magnificent vessels made from lapis lazuli. Blood from a toad. Just before dawn. Amusing mazurkas. Custard apples. He basks in sunlight bouncing off the moon. Cancer in his brains. Kicking dogs in his sleep. Give me back those pages. Wrinkled between doubts. Drastic and measured. Each type of pepper burns a different place on the tongue. The photos came back. He looks sad in every pose. Full of thoughts. Stripes on walls. Confession has never helped. Eyes speak volumes. A pair of bandits fighting over the spoils. Even prayer books were stolen and pawned. Nasty fucks from behind. Greasy footprints with clumps of fur. He sent blank postcards. Double doors made of iron bars. Spider webs. Unbearable secrets are ringed and weighted down with lead. Rickety larks. Maybe nothing at all. I found a simple exit. I carried them through it with the gloom of a man who has just escaped great danger. Choirs droned. No two voices breathed at the same instant. Soft slurs and hushed hisses. Drumbeats drove away enemies. Every word uttered is heard at the top of the spiral. Single sentences alternate between masculine and feminine rhymes. Jet-lagged applause. Lacking vitamins. I have the runs. Another disappointed marathon. No wonder. Just agenda. Bourbon. Low-key monogamy. Shaved head. Lazy drama. Sexual peek-a-boo. The cheating unkind. As if I didn't know what goes on in condos. Crimps in curtains. Perfect time. Online nags. Three-hour nap. Goes in easy. Solid chunks. Second talk. Gentle silly. Slick and saucy. Sit down on my quotes. Why the single tear? I have a passion for prefaces. I hate so many things. Each a different way. As many varieties as there are kinds of love. My tendons hurt. I wanted to create the most amoral person. Nothing to do with madness. Two snorts of coke and plain boiled yams. I'm afraid to go out. There are fantasies of running down anonymous pedestrians with his car. Desperate blood and weekend guts. A mountain of wheat sewn into his linings lets the peaches rot in the bin. Paranoia in such detail. I bought a series of miniatures. Nude portraits of black angels. He squeezed with all his might. Nothing else came out. The stubborn and cruel lottery of mornings. I used a circular deck. Cards fanned out around me. Reading the flights of small birds and scattering mice. Only he can take it the way I dish it out. Side orders of macaroni and cheese. Clay kingdoms rich in diamonds. Heavy horns protrude from his forehead. Rows of corn. The fat braids of a connoisseur. Spangles from a ruined palace. Tilted squares of cedar wood channel wind into every building. Projectiles of sand pockmarked the silver coffins. I hid. Desperate in his natural caves. So begins the journey through a lifetime of pictures, procedures and permutations. Leftover among poor curiosities. Knotty. Lighting fires in fireplaces. Made of my father's unpolished stones. Snap and crackle. Old flames pop. Kindling tied down by caring. I used to take sides with the part of me that cried. This required little thoughts. He held my hand under tables. No one can take you where you need to be going. In sleep I leave everyone behind. Muffled sparks. Yellow chalk circles washed away in lather. Lists of wicks. Abandoned shades. Engaged under the light of his favorite lamp. Faces were reproduced exactly. He accommodated blemish. Conning elegant ideas from old books. Likenesses suited their imposing frames. Whole feasts on the end of one spoon. Shoveling good tastes onto a rascal's tongue. The best tarts come when half the plums are firm and sour. Fortune smiles. A millionaire's teeth are missing. The hits. Not the kisses. Contemplating rump. He could still feel the warmth on his cheeks. Soon to be a sequined corpse. A gored marquis dining on chimeras. Crouched on the brink of vengeance. I see less satisfying visions. A grave-digger takes off his black shoes. He's digging life-sized holes in walls of earth. An arm hangs from one of the holes. A bandage the color of his skin is wrapped around the pinky finger. The thumb is in shadow. This makes the hand appear as a claw. The hand flexes and moves upwards as the arm curves. It is the delicate smooth hand of a young man. He is dressed in a white suit. There is no dirt on his clothes. He rubs his forehead and touches his shaved head. He tries to sit up, but is held in place by woven medical restraints. More struggling against the straps proves futile. The gravedigger is an older man, wearing black pants and a black turtleneck sweater. He reaches inside the hole and caresses the re-strained man's ankle through his sock. They exchange a few words that have a calming effect on both of them. The grave-digger walks off through rows of folding chairs into miles of desert. One by one, people arrive and sit in the folding chairs. They are well dressed. The man in the wall starts to shake and fight against the restraints. His eyes are closed, but he seems overwhelmed by the audience that is assembling in front of him. A closed circuit video camera is pointing at him. The little red light is on. It's watching and recording the struggle. A man in a gray suit comes up to the hole in the wall. He gives the young man a shot in the arm with a sy-ringe and holds his hand until the struggling stops. The audi-ence applauds. They sent me home in a limo. The driver was handsome. Innocent vanity. Dire and straight. I tried to catch his eyes in the rearview mirror. Is it worth the trouble to imagine the future? The sense of predestination accompa-nies certain tongued preludes. I have become my own ex-periment. How much can I change myself? Breaking down a ridge of vermilion wax. A rude rim between adjoining spheres. He said I was a little devil. Jerk chicken and hot fudge. Someone saw us. Spectacles of ourselves. Someone has to read it. Someone who doesn't know me. That's almost everybody. I learned how to rebuild in different ways. Returning to a rejected form after many idle days. Honeyed hexagrams. Sublime precepts for deaf fears. Scholarly expenditures in his wallet. At which juncture does life become untangling? Dunno. Settle in and let the worms do it. You know. When your orifices are drying up and your face is carbon paper drying on bone. He said never believe in the one celestial chord. Beauty doesn't come in black and white. Human beings still try to be the emotional centers of every picture. My moods are the vestiges and projections of erratic laboratory particles on his monitor. He put them in the background but can't finally remove them. There are bright blue skies. A single tern soars over the gleaming pinks of wet sand. And milk crates full of crumpled florescent beach clothes. An outlandish collection of rubber toys made to float. Half-inflated mermaids with starfish eyes. Necklaces of iridescent shells and bits of coral. Aqua dolphins. Plastic pail and shovel. It takes twenty tints from a single broken color to make the pale mist that rises from crashing waves. Not side by side, but overlaid like patient spirits caught in a hand-blown shot glass. Poured from a rock crystal juglet adorned with a raised foliage motif. The anger of last week has vanished. I want to wear shorts and frolic. But the rain keeps me indoors. My thoughts run sideways when I'm alone. In and out of the same loops. Expanding the pool from which codes are constructed. That's been a colossal distraction for years. I've stashed myself in sites of difficult access. Firewalls present no hurdles to the invaders. I invent a fragile comfort in the intricate arcades far above me. Really I might as well be in a cardboard tent, but I retain a mania for mechanical expertise. I bought a new backpack just in case. Even full, it can't be heavier than the dregs of human affection. Where is that passage into graceful old age? The interplay of technology and violence. An interactive promo. Holding on to dangerous contradictions seems necessary. He doesn't get sore anymore. I tell him to close his eyes and concentrate on the sensations. He says he sees a square section of ordinary concrete. It's gray and coarse. In the center is an oval of a darker gray than the rest of the concrete. The oval is pockmarked and has flaking beige patches near the center. It looks as if the removal of a sign caused the pockmarks and discoloration. Above the oval is a pipe sticking out. A small rectangular object dangles from a white cable. The object looks like a small television screen, but it could just be a piece of gray metal with a frame around it. It hangs just inside the top of the oval. To the right of the pipe is a small glass lamp. It is a distorted cube with the top of the cube larger than the bottom. A decorative ring sits on top. The lamp is attached to a round disk that in turn is attached to the concrete. The glass of the lamp is darkened. It is unclear whether this lamp functions or if it has a bulb inside it. Shadows fall diagonally across the wall, probably caused by the afternoon sun. Spindly shadow lines reach inside the oval. It is unclear what is out of sight, causing the shadows. A tree? Perhaps some machinery? The other shadow shapes from the pipe, lamp, and the television screen are much larger than the objects themselves and stretched so they don't resemble the objects that determine them. He's wide-awake. Enjoying this reversal.

He tells me to open my eyes. I tell him most people see what they already know. He smiles. Through the window behind him I see the statues that line the half-circle of driveway in front of this house. They are poorly sculpted and of inferior stone. There is a similar inscription on tarnished copper plaques below each one. A young man weeping. A bearded old man laughing. Hunchbacked. A peasant woman with a grimy bosom. A deformed child of indeterminate sex. No gods or goddesses left on these pedestals. Long ago they slipped out of view in a caravan of budget rental cars. Glove compartments stashed with guns and contracts. Objects made of numbers and light have taken over. He could still be carried away by the thrill of his own verbal acrobatics. He spoke as if he was standing in front of a full-length mirror. Feverish stories poured out of his pale dripping face. Frequently, he pressed his fingertips to his throat to feel the resonance of his voice. He stopped mid-sentence. I thought he had sensed me watching him though the open doorway. I felt sure he would never know the pleasure of listening. He was too practiced at hiding thoughts. His gaze fixed on the wall before him. He had discovered a large moth the same ash gray as the wall. Asleep. Clinging there on the concrete. He folded the pages of his stories into a flat tube and raised it clenched in his fist. As he swung, the moth detached itself and zig-zagged up to the ceiling. He chased it, swinging the bundle of words haphazardly above his head. The furry insect landed on a pleated lampshade. Its wings beating for a moment before it became still. No doubt feeling the bright warm pull of the naked bulb a few inches away. His giddy swats knocked the lamp to the floor. The yellow light shot out of the crushed shade, illuminating a fan-shaped section of a finely woven carpet. A broad tree trunk with flat snakes knotted around it. Slender knives of green clasped in their teeth. Heads sprouted from huge blossoms. Dragons and daredevils. Denizens and dervishes. Everyone keeps making the same mistakes. Darlings. I am afraid of living life around a disease. The backs of my legs were sunburned. One ankle was swollen. He made shade with a beach towel and a couple of branches. While I hid from the sun, he ran in the waves. Later, he rubbed vinegar on my skin. He blew off a brunch to watch me peel. I can't turn down someone who wants to play infuriating games. He liked to smell things while blindfolded. From expensive shops. Grapefruit and hot horses. Latex florets dusted with talc. On each of his nipples I dabbed peach pit oil tinted with a fusion of scents designed for both men and women. I handcuffed his scarred wrists behind his back. Forced him to his knees. He inhaled chocolate chip cookie dough from a charred wooden spoon. Candied orange peel and brandied pear fused with the tears and mink oil he'd rubbed into my leathers. I took a photograph, but he saw the flash. He thought it was lightning. Another flash flood raging outdoors. I kept him nervous and eager. I dreamt of polka dots that changed colors when they stung people. The victims went into comas. Pie tins. A field strewn with identical bronze shards. Each engraved with hazy pictograms and pairs of tiny lovebirds. I wish I had recorded those sessions. Residual bits of his ideas stuck in dusty corners. He thought he was not pleasing me enough. He crawled around under cars in the parking lot as a punishment and began to write the same sentence over and over holding a pencil in his mouth. I stood on his arms until he calmed down. Cruelty can be a special gift between the right people. Mostly it's not done well. A badge is not a shield. My fan was taxed in the wretched heat. If you don't know how far away something is, there's no way to know how fast it's moving. He was patient. He identified seagulls, jet fighters, and the reflections of ceiling lights in photographs taken through windows. Another bright-eyed boy with a few too many drinks in him. I gave him the first knuckle of my fuck finger. I have become the kind of journalist that strays from informing his readers in order to draw attention to himself. He loves to criticize me for that. What is a happy death anyhow? He used to be a feminist hairdresser. Always unable to luxuriate in the joy of shopping. Gas mask or snake bite kit. Zeroing in on better decisions. It hurts to dig out what's been buried so deep. He made sculptures that looked like warts. I threw up in the cab home. Nightfall. Gnarled visions welled up inside. Despite his will. There are no treaties with monsters. He trusted flukes. In his basement. Unrepentant pigs. Batty women walked around wrapped in sheets. Bitter melon. Quinine or delirium. Perverted patrons thrilled by fresh talent. Pushing their conservative crayon flora behind his malicious mockingbirds and feisty rattlers. Too gory, they thought, for modern walls. People expect to see dead bodies transfixed with bent wires. Posed and poised. All cleaned up. A bit of sealing wax and string. Framed and over-lit. Pretty rows. There's such a demand after something vile gets tagged and discussed in print. Few among us live for the unresolved. Imagine no possible direction. Try to make mistakes. Curious phenomena flourish in the absence of expectation. He had a slight lisp. He walked his dog every day in the park. I can't separate these things. Someone needs to lubricate his political frontier. A rape machine. Forever kissing babies. Moving his office

89

uptown. He likes to sleep on the couch there. Among misspelled names he can't pronounce. The waitress had skintight blue jeans and dried snot hanging out of her nose. He told me I had beautiful eyes. The bagel arrived upside down to hide the burned part. I gave him a box of magnetic dirty words. He put on thick glasses and slicked back his hair with pomade. We stayed together because we didn't cater to love. Games of chance were not permitted. The city enchanted him and he lost all of his money anyway. He took snapshots that hint at possible delights. I fell back into the labyrinth of his untutored imagination. More secret chambers emptied of custom. Good roofers are hard to come by these days. I put hooks in the four corners of my closet. Burgers and a bath together. His soapy fingers in my mouth. I watched him unpack and put books on the shelves. I memorized the titles. If you wash the nipples, the pups don't suck. Line by line, the picture takes shape. Nothing but sand and rock. Where are the lights of civilization? Certain things are more important than others. You're a genius and the rest of us just write garbage. He couldn't sleep without earplugs. The grumpy treatment. Bad politics makes good business. Go over it again and again until the excitement is gone. Is that why they call it monogamy? We left doors open between us when we were in separate rooms. Showing respect for others' vocabulary levels is a basic element of fair play. He said I must first read the classics. Until that moment, I thought ogres didn't read the classics. It's so difficult to combine delicacy with satire. And I'm horny as hell. His thoughts look like cat toys. He's afraid of poverty. Quibbling about the phone bill. Can't we just read a lot of things and challenge each other? A mosaic of lies might at least be beautiful. Hours without electricity. No more talk about celebrity. He sat on the floor amid fragments of melting ice. A screwdriver in his hand. The milk had soured. Brittle days. Show down or let down. I will find a way to make friends with him. I kissed him on the forehead. White. Skeletal birches. His eyebrows looked like two drawn swords. An unwavering being at home in his workshop. Pegboard with tools hanging on hooks. Peach crates filled with brown paper bags of nails and screws. Drums of grease for the farm machinery. Odd containers from a factory. Overgrown vines. Treacherous roads after dark. Bizarre antics played out in the reconstructed past of the designer. Don't amputate something you will need later. I fell into a river once trying to leap from one stone to another. A big wet hug. Something that can heal. Change the sensing parameters of the radar. Tenderness expresses itself through consonants that correspond to the sucking movement of lips. He was hungry and needed cigarettes. These reunions were my theater. Sudden recognition awakens remorse. The broom that sweeps the cobwebs away. Favorite haunts. Fluid masterpieces. A coffin always reopened. Nineteen pieces of folded white paper are held in place with nineteen rocks the size of a fist or smaller. They sit in a patch of earth, making a rough oval eight feet tall and three feet wide. Clumps of grass grow around the oval. A few small clumps are growing inside it. Near the stone farthest away, are two foot-long cylinders lying next to each other. They are white. The color of the folded papers. A green vase made of an opaque material rests next to the cylinders. It holds a single pink star-shaped flower with white edges. In his country dalliance is shrouded in mystery. His eyes speak a perfected seductive language. Two together are always going somewhere. I just want to wander. Forgery is not an issue. Copies are made by tracing or with the original alongside. He makes it sound wonderful. I could get lost in controlling him. What exactly happened that night? Don't harp on the crummy parts. Look, someone has to do these things. Don't get freaked out by intimacy. One letter away. We don't have to live with that sappy stuff. Congratulations on your new addition. Think only of others during your stay. Idolizing idleness. Do not disturb. Profit from your talents. Most of my pieces are full of holes. My little woodworm. They are hung on walls anyway. I've entered my most regulated period. Stop hiding behind decoration. Separate out the rage. Spit it out onto gold-speckled parchment. Its value is estimated by the number of notations that are added afterwards. Namesakes in shuttle-shaped cartouches. Gelatinous ancestors with a fanatical belief in nothingness. The world tolerates weirdos only on its own terms. So go on. Keep up those appearances. Sold out shows seven days a week for a hundred lifetimes. A steamer trunk of crossed out days. A perfumed sudoku anthology on every shelf where the literary journals used to be. In philosophy there is never any new data. Valiant efforts in tight pants. Publicity stunts growth. Oh come now. He wasn't ashamed. He thought only of amusing himself and filled his pockets with sweets. Dressed for the opera. Four hundred dollars on a thin calfskin coat that won't get him through his first winter here. The elegiac note was unmistakable. He claimed his true pleasure in smoking came from the sight of the smoke. Only the most expensive tobacco escaped from the corners of his mouth at precise intervals. It reminded me of the curlicues on illuminated manuscripts. I wondered if the old masters could prolong these giddy arabesques into pages of senseless spinning. Chasing their tails with angled nib and burnt beeswax. Two men sit in a café. The younger one is telling a story. A few tears are dripping down his face. Behind them a waiter is stacking chairs on table. The manager is counting the till money. He rolls the bills and puts rubber bands around them. The young man is sobbing now. The older one listening is irritated but nods his head every so often in sympathy. The young man puts his head against the older man's shoulder for a moment, but immediately jerks away and stands up. He exits the café without another word. The older man goes to the counter and searches through his wallet. He hands the manager a bill and walks outside without waiting for change. The young man takes deep breaths of the night air. They walk together along an uneven sidewalk. Movie posters are pasted on plywood panels that line the street. They enter another café and order drinks at a table. Two men come into the café and stand near them. They laugh and point at the young man. He starts crying again and the older man leads him out of the café. They stand in front of the entrance to an underground station. The young man is quite drunk. He's sobbing again. He puts his hand around the neck of the older man and pulls his head closer. Their lips meet in a simple kiss. They pat each other's backs. The young man pushes himself away and stumbles down the concrete stairs backwards. He catches hold of the handrail, turns around, and continues down the stairs into the orange light of the station tunnel below. The house lights came up and we were the only ones not applauding. His hand was still in my lap. The old tart next to me pretended we weren't there. She had an orchid pinned to her dress. The color of his skin when it bruises. I wanted to tell her his whole basement was

93

full of orchids. Under special spotlights. I smacked the spunk right out of him. He said the tenor was shrill. There could have been less moaning and shrieking. What is it like to wait without being able to move? A bunch of short things fastened together into one long thing. Tell it to me from that perspective. Risk-taking becomes more important. There are happy atheists you know. It's easy to mock someone's trust in a pilgrimage. Just don't wallow in the excesses of despair. His drugs made him fuzzier. I ate some ribs and set the alarm. He worried that his feminine attributes were obvious to everyone. Perhaps, that's why he kept the apartment so cold. He was seized by a whim I found repugnant. He introduced numbers as a means of identification. Digital tags were placed on furniture, utensils, knickknacks, and body parts. I preferred the solidity of primes well above zero. What would a nation of atheists be like? He couldn't decide where to put the decimal points. I told him he was more girlish than boyish at times. He showed up later drunk and a little something else. It's tough being a bastard and being appreciated all the time. His beauty stood motionless and upright without any sense of fatigue. I hoped it wouldn't leak into my dreams. Quiet simmering violence left me out of breath. I heard a famous author read who didn't know how to pronounce big words. Still, I laughed the whole time at his wit. The intent to delete the message remains evident. The fingers and eyes of the reader caress the creases and wrinkles. Can paperless mail be crumpled? Are we always grateful enough for speed? It's more dangerous these days to go slow, to stop and move backwards. Speculative fiction in reverse. Gather instead of plant. Give up bones for stones. Looking for dark mirrors in either direction. I made lemonade and held him while he fought me and everything else in his sleep. Soft caramel centers. Worlds apart. I never stopped looking for innovative alternatives. The careful arrangement of a bouquet into a slender crystal vase. New recipes for the same old dishes. A sense of progress is evident, but less so than reported. Technical skills are overrated in making the kind of discoveries I crave. I am lost inside a vast labyrinth of words and images. Black curving lines are spread unevenly across the concrete under my feet. My shoe bottoms leave ebony-mirrored blots in the shiny adhesive liquid. The intersecting loops and coils are similar to drawings that chart the complex paths subatomic particles take during contained reactions. There's a sliver of dirt between the concrete's rough edge and a lighter grayish concrete barrier. There is one pair of arrows spray-painted in orange on the barrier. They are the marks that workmen make before they dig up the streets. There's a long thin metal piece lying in the dirt. It has five unequal segments. Each is demarcated with a narrow band of white paint made from pulverized seashells. His eyes jerked back and forth under clenched lids. He had once been a knife that cut through anything. I accepted the rotten moods as part of his cycle of highs and lows and lower stills. Tulips. Wilted and mottled. Wrapped in marbled tissue. Out and out buffoonery. Unhappy accidents of character. Lemons and onions. Peeled, chopped, and burnt on an iron skillet. Crab claws. Stag horns. Pepper dots. Tangled hemp. Cloud heads. Splashed ink. Scandalous pranks. Veins in a lotus leaf. Eyes of polished obsidian. A conversation with long silences. New theories about tides. He took a ceramic mug from my kitchen cabinet and washed it with soapy water before using it. I wasn't prepared for contempt. He thought it okay to scorn the mediocre. No brain is as elastic as a child's before it's mired in dogma and intolerance. Some things sneak up on me. They emerge on my palette of desires. It becomes impossible to shut them out. There is a lessening, but nothing I do makes them go away. It makes me wonder if I can ever make contact with anyone here again. Maybe I never have. I find I can only touch the blurred edges where colors meet and become indistinct. There is an emptiness that lives with me in ambiguous locations. He fell asleep pressed against me. Mouth open. Pulling whatever stuck out into his dream. His hands crossed above his head as if they were tied there. I was wide-awake and dead to the world. He wore my shirt the whole weekend. I amused myself with eccentricities. He spent hours reading how charlatans deceived the credulous. Naming alter egos to express opposing viewpoints. Some pictures are never complete. They are constructed over the course of centuries by the combined efforts of a succession of thinkers. He traveled as much as possible. Trying to curry favor. Stopovers in luxurious hotels once frequented by wealthy artisans. In a lobby of jade and jasper he was captivated by a faded fresco of tilted triangles. Curly worms ate away at the integrity of straight edges. Upon closer inspection, he saw they were ravenous rows of numbers. Conventions once smeared on dusted planks returned by scratching wax or clay. Days later, on dewy hillsides he found these intricate ciphers coiled in the prayers and melodies of lonely shepherds. The tips of his fingernails were already black as he handed me a pewter snuffbox. He wanted to teach me how to grow rich from any mob's love of amusement. Some ravens have taught themselves how to bark. I told him I had settled for a few free copies of my words coming back at me in the mail. We parted early and I felt his best interests taunting me. I attended a poetry reading in a leaky art gallery. Dreary lifeless thoughts hitting the walls. Slapping a side of beef. The gallery owner went from person to person asking if they were poets. Doesn't everyone write poems? Not anymore. The state just runs around putting swords into the hands of madmen, while the peasants are self-helping themselves to death. Something about the weather. Sleet. Or snow and rain. Mixed. Squiggly lines organized into groups that transmit ideas from brain to brain. Drop wet spaghetti on the floor. It bounces all over the place. I like it when it means different things at different moments. Or even at the same time. Most people look for stabilizing markers. The four corners of every room. Completeness and permanence. Huh? They keep rearranging the same cages. He thought I was bored. He spent hours snubbing out-of-towners at parties. His insults were flawless. Quite correctly measured cubes of manure. Packed into the cheap compartments of vivid blue ice trays. Paint fumes made him sick. Time and tiredness modulated how I saw his colors. I deleted features that exhausted me. Afterimages lingered long enough to influence how I fabricated the next object. I filled history with fairy tales to make it more interesting. Steamed omasum and mushrooms braised in thin strips of ginger. He learned about color from watching rainbows and shining lights on the feathers of his birds. He wanted to get a dog to keep him company. I'd settle for a great many card games. Shuffling show-offs and moist cigars. Five little girls who dress like their mothers. Prose pregnant with hemistiches. Unintentional verse in a speech makes a bad impression. We fought over the shade of wall paint. Papaya with tapioca pearl. Nothing stabilized him.

More pointless shrieks. The most brilliant reds were made from hard-shelled vermin. Hand-picked from columns of converted fish tanks. I liked him better when he was drunk. He came to life. I never knew whose. I couldn't afford the deep-end of his pool. The continual revulsion towards decent things. The total movement that comes from the death of routine. Here, an overture protrudes into the audience as novel architecture. Instruments lurching outward together in violent motions. Pulled by the conductor's hidden strings. I was jerking off when he called to apologize. He was perplexed and worried about my silence. I said I didn't have time to go with him to buy paint. I couldn't tell him I had abandoned color. I was setting up screens. Making a shape I had never seen to hide behind. I reorganized, cleaned, swept, threw out, only to realize later that I had concealed most of the tools necessary to continue. A table. Black. Either metal or wood. Butts up against a brick wall. A layer of black paint is peeling off the brick in many places. The bright colors of older layers are visible underneath. Silver. Bright red. Deep blue. The ceiling and the floor are not visible. On the table a young man is lying on his back. He is nude except for a black posing strap. His body is meticulously sculpted. His head rests on a black pillow scrunched up against the brick where the table touches the wall. His bare feet rest three feet apart on a shiny metal bar that is situated twenty inches above the edge of the table, parallel to it. With his legs bent up in this position, his hairless ass is spread apart. The contents of the posing strap's pouch are held neatly out of the way above the glistening pucker that contracts and expands slightly, perhaps in accordance with some predetermined instruction or by direction from the older man who stands beside the table.

The older man wears clothes made from the same shiny rubber as the pillowcase and the younger man's strap. Only his head remains uncovered. He squirts gobs of a white greasy substance from a tube and carefully coats the surface of both latex-covered hands. His hands and lower arms appear unnaturally puffy as if he stirred up a beehive with them only moments ago. Slowly, he massages the three central fingers of his left hand into the accommodating portal that continues to pulse upon entry. The young man clasps his hands behind his head. His unblinking eyes look up into the face of the older man as he accepts the fourth finger. The thumb tip added to the fingertips makes a moist star. A gasp as knuckles disappear. Then again minutes later as the widest girth of the hand slips beyond sight. Much more slowly, the older man begins to insert the fingers of his right hand on top of his left wrist. As the right hand slides forward the left one retracts. Followed by the reverse. Over and over the older man exchanges one hand for the other inside the young man. On the other side of the brick wall. An enormous metal storage container. Painted black. There is a long opening in the metal. A rectangle about three feet tall and six inches wide. A pale loaf of bread, a selection of dinner rolls, some dusted with flour and seeds on top, poke out of this opening. The asphalt paving underneath is cracked and crumbling. Small pieces of brick and stone are scattered about. The brick wall is old and has graffiti on it. Unreadable words. A thick circle painted in yellow. Two spray-painted arrows pointing away from two cylindrical shapes that look like drums on their sides. They are white. To the left of the old brick is a section of wall in a lighter red color. The mortar is fresh. The brick clean, unmarked. A woman's upper body and head sit on the sidewalk near the newer wall. She appears to be made of fine white stone, but is splattered with a rust-colored substance. Or she could be made of iron that has been colored white. The speckles could actually be rust. She has no arms, but she's wearing a dress with a neckline that rides just above her petite buttressed breasts. One pearled button of her dress is perched off-center in the cleavage between them. She wears an undergarment that comes up about two inches from behind the top of her dress. This slip has a squared neckline with a thick border that appears to be embroidered. The material below the neckline is bunched and wavy. She seems to be bursting out of the dress, as if the dress is peeling away. Her hair is parted in the middle and pulled back. An open rose rests on her hair above two curly strands of unequal length and thickness that trail down the center of her forehead. Her eyes are open, not wide. She is just to the right of where I am standing. Her mouth neither smiles nor frowns, but the expression on her face implies a resigned weariness. The brownish orange splattering is unevenly spread on her face. Most of it is just above the eyes, on the front of her chin, and on the left cheek. Perhaps that lends to the overall impression of displeasure I feel from her. But she still holds herself in a regal manner, as if nothing could make her ugly or humiliated. This bust is not more than a foot wide and eighteen inches tall. The foreground of the sidewalk is made of gray concrete with pebbles embedded in it. She rests just behind a seam between that foreground and the part of the sidewalk behind that is lighter gray and has no pebbles. Behind her, leaning against the brick, is an unpainted wrought-iron grill of softly rounded spirals and leaf shapes. There is a flattened soft drink cup to the left of her and next to that, a slender paper sleeve that still retains the shape of the plastic straw that it used to hold. Above her head is a white rectangle that is not recognizable as anything but a white rectangle. Perhaps it used to be a sign. I kept pressing it to feel the soreness. The swollen gland on my neck. I missed his middle of the night phone calls. The lackluster performances. The phantom tree house that reason couldn't find. I had to stop trying to fix him. Spur of the moment missionary work is patting oneself on the back. Pretend mending. Every gesture is magnified. Lights out. Whiskery protuberances wiggled on glass slides. Cylindrical shields resembling overwrought meanings. He'll never stop using me to cause him pain. What does it take to knock something that big out of its orbit? The whole machine lost in a great crowd of ranting magpies. He knew how to eat without hunger. To avoid reading my letters. To waste time and energy searching for decoys. A flutter of wings and he was gone. Leaving me a stone. Rare gases tightly held within a crustal hull. I bought a copy and had him sign it. Hundreds of tiny corpses with blood on their beaks. Death and glory boys. At his feet. And still. Such skilled spelunking. That slippery void the shape of a pickle. Milking it for publicity. The least likely candidate in one of our best journals. I ran laps behind him. Flat ovals. Rank sneaker in the showers. It was freezing cold. Maybe I stopped loving mountains. Maybe I climbed the wrong ones. The peaks all hovered in my head. Blended together. Each had the same name. He did, too. A rocky road for one. Sensible shoes. I read the verses he liked and saw how words cling and clang. I listened to the wireless at odd hours. More stupid songs for suckers. An ear to the door. Again the rustle of wings. Data eventually suggests too many differences. I stayed. Itchy. I must have been fucking nuts. Flowery sentences shooting out of me. Beastly banter. Every which way. Muster of peacocks. Paraffin on embers. Pig and pepper. Pale underparts. I played etudes on his upright. The melody rose quietly in the left hand. One story after another at full volume. Daily expenditure. Improvised meals. Adventures in supermarkets. Candy corn and fish sticks. He was on to something. Maybe it was right. The check-out line. It was good to lose. For a while. Having an audience would have helped me learn how to win. Layers of sediment transformed by increasing pressure. Ropes dangling from his ceiling. Legs horizontal. Six pack. Hand over hand. He wouldn't meet my friends. I wasn't allowed to meet his. He was out there somewhere. Blasted with ecstasy. Smoking cheap fags. Snorting ambergris. Thumping cassava. I ridiculed his ideas. His salty gargles. A snail fattened on milk. Woodpeckers in pickup trucks. Let him be. He's just preoccupied. Taking a course in coarse alchemy. Busting up the household gods for firewood. Taming the fleshed-out savages he once fondled in children's books. Eventually, blood brothers and battleaxes are buried in the same grave. Floral whorls in multiples of five. Worn down captions on the upper registers of limestone reliefs. Drifters on the surface film of quiet ponds. The best sleep protected by morning light. Sooner or later mining dreams is an underhanded enterprise. Tinny music and horse droppings. He had a bourgeois mind. Everything had to be twisted before it was of any use. Smoke. Kerosene. Raw onions Mothballs. How unfair to open doors on rooms without light and shove someone's feelings into them. I kept him up late at night. Staring into smoldering fires. He collected bottle caps and laughed until he was sore. He picked a fight with his own image reflected in a window. I figured things out. Getting and giving. Stuttering and sputtering over buried treasure. Silver flying cranes painted on a lead bridge. Weaknesses exposed. All this recording of transitions. Emblems of personal cultivation. Eyes on the composite object and its many ridiculous ingredients. It's terribly sweet in there. I said he was a series of rather flimsy concentric circles. He said I was a shit. Watch out. Don't settle for the subtle approach. That particular shade of delicacy. A glutton for punishment. Bastinado in a bungalow. Hissing contentedly. A charge of gunpowder. Gasoline and vinegar. A remedy against those long nights. One was orange with black borders. Another black with orange and scarlet edges. Enormous patches of metallic blue luster. Honeydew secretions relished by welcome guests. I gave up the idea of preserving exactness. A moon pulling frothy water across beaches. Leaving slimy greens and browns half-covered in the smooth sand. New pictures gave no solid evidence of an ocean ever existing there. I had hunted so long for isolated hot spots in a continent of glaciers. Blanketed hideaways of exultant and ruthless noise. Seizures in which inhibition falls away. I marked him up good. Unaware of the long-term effect he was having on me. Tortoiseshell safari. Inked on his thighs. A dissertation on grindstones. Engraved on his backside. The over-refinement of oracles. Erupting inside his tender throat. Guided tours of the underground. He blushed beneath it all. Corners waiting to be tucked under mattresses. Processes that must be fulfilled in impressionable receptacles. Bloodshot eyes peer out from a looming repository of deeds. Carved into the tusk tips that serve as handles for fly-whisks. Oily rags piled in rusted buckets all over town. Spontaneous combustion in broom closets.

A hand-bound notebook with a brown leather cover. Open and pages facing down. Tubes of epoxy. Masking tape. Balls of twine. A circular saw propped up in a diagonal to the tabletop where it rests. The base of the saw is hidden by a crumpled white packing material that is bunched around it. On the floor are several two-by-fours of varying lengths. They are piled unevenly. The tips are spray-painted key-lime green. To the left of the wood sits a dirty white plastic bucket and a large bag of a white powdery substance. The powder dusts the top of the bag where it is torn open. Other items in foreground are impossible to identify. The back wall of this room is made of bricks, but they are strangely wavy and warped as if seen through an old windowpane. There are two large white squares on the wall. Their blurry edges suggest they are not actually on the wall, but are in fact much smaller and hang over the plastic bucket a few inches in front of the wall. They are not at right angles to the floor and walls. They are skewed one above and to the right of the other one. They appear to be the same size. To the left is a sloppily wound coil of plastic-coated wire and a wooden crate that used to hold beer bottles. A boy sits on it. Perhaps seven years old. He's wearing baggy denim jeans and a red sports jersey of some sort. A blue baseball cap with some lettering on it. He has one hand held in front of him. Open, as if he's trying to get someone's attention. His other hand is clenched and pointed at the floor between his legs. His fist is not screwed in place properly. It is larger than his other unclenched hand and stuck onto his arm in such a way that it must have been taken from an adult-sized mannequin. His eyes stare into the street through the warped windowpane. Reflected buildings and the windows in them obscure the words on his cap and jersey and make miniature rectangles that hover over his face. A young man in a police uniform comes out of the one of the buildings. He crosses the street and walks past the boy who stares straight ahead. Never moving. The young man enters another building and walks down a long dim hallway. He tilts his head as if he's listening to something in front of him. He slows down as he approaches a doorway. His hand is on the gun in the holster strapped to his leg. His shoes and the cuffs of his pants are covered in white powder. He enters an old room. A wallpaper grid of red diamonds is cracked and faded from years of sunlight. Each diamond frames the same two intertwined white lilies inside it. A wrinkled man with white hair sits in the room's only chair near the only window. It's wide open. He's holding a slim hardcover book. He offers it to the young policeman. The officer takes the book and opens it to a page with an oval portrait of the author. He closes the book and slips the volume into the pocket of his uniform shirt. The old man stands up and the officer helps him put on his tattered jacket before escorting him out of the room into the dim hallway. He told me I didn't pay enough attention to dreams. I said the alarm clock destroys them all. The radio voices spew news all over the remnants. A few little shapes linger. An activity. A face. A feeling of dread or warmth. Never enough to puzzle over. Maybe I don't like dreams. Maybe I want to get cozy with the thoughts I'm trying to control. Perchance. He had a platitudinous mom. He felt stupid when he was sober. Cloudy skies. Empty stretches of road. A pale globe whirling in a field of trodden wildflowers. A briefcase full of wrongs. Least likely to succeed. When did courage die? Why focus on the little rifts? Simple problems led him to such serious difficulties.

Stopped dead in his tracks. His disease was about maintaining distances. Building secret societies and bombs. They printed my stories word for word. I wouldn't call them dreams. I wouldn't call them anything at all. Cans of worms. The kind that sting and bite. Queasy stomach. The underlying pitter pats. The nurse gives me a shot. Hatred is manageable. It can be perfected over time. It has to be pulled out regularly and looked at with discerning eyes. Dark chocolate sauce over ice cream. Ping pong. Parks and cafes. I bathed him and made him coffee he didn't drink. No hotels. No rental car. I remained a foreigner in my own country. Remaindered in the boondocks. The exiled air sits heavy in the lungs. He left weird messages exhaled in abandoned houses. I took to climbing the mountains again. Gasping thinner atmospheres. Resting in crags. I held a terracotta vessel. Heartbeats throbbed in my fingers. An inner shelf divided two equal chambers. I heard starving mice crawl from one to the other. Their skittish motions disturbing the brittle bones of finches they had gnawed clean earlier. They licked the flour I had sprinkled there. I let them scamper down my arms and legs to find comfort under damp stones. I stared at the bones. Noting features of their configuration. Suspicious of the calm. I went back down. Crunching through frozen puddles. I forgave him every uncalled for cruelty. Made light of it. Smelled his stink and thought it my own. Bathing in my own furious exclusion. Alphabets formed on twirling plates. Teetering. Holding his finger under my nostrils. I drew out his blood and mixed it with mine in the sand of an hourglass. The uneven tide had come so quickly and feelings took their time going away. We each drew maps on the other's back. They led us to different countries under the same stars. Two zodiacs with entirely different symbols. Each broken down into a number of distinctive sounds. I lost myself in composition. He simply lost it. A rough figure. Unpainted. Chisel marks emphasized. Take your medication. No, the purple ones with the smiley faces. Dictate your own nightmares into agreeable machines. Death is already implicit in the situation. Scapegoat reruns in every living room. Order images from a menu. Beer and bastards. Every choice was the same. I closed my eyes and saw the afterimages from the screens. The barks of his terrier. The paw prints. The chewed shoes. The slobber. The poop. I filled in plumbing diagrams with details. I realized I would never come clean. Grueling interviews. Strictly business. He wanted to do suburban things in empty barns. He even prayed before dinner. I once had invisible friends. They lived in folded sheets. Stitched together and placed between thin wooden boards. They spoke a highly refined gibberish between pencil sketches of old cutlery. I did finally learn to talk back. Pots of jasmine tea. Green buds bursting open. Releasing two dried white flowers in the hot water. A dance of silken veils. Encrypting new olfactory sensations. He wanted to practice objective fidelity in capturing the physical world. Silly me. Thinking I was finished with all that movable type. I couldn't touch him. I didn't want to settle for stenciling. He pressed on despite his minor feelings. Celebrating even the unwelcome aspects of travel. He cleared his throat and went to bed at a reasonable hour. I lay awake thinking impossible things. Poised over treacherous whirlpools. Hours before eggs and toast. Elderberry jam. There is no love without some kind of role-playing. Not integrated. Affectionate theater seating for some higher purpose. That's a definite no-no. Special amplifying equipment not allowed.

Elevated states. Thirteenth floor. I must have had an inflamed conscience. Without the high heels. Overwhelmed by the twinkling from dead stars. Slender needles pierced a drifting viewpoint. An infusion of laudanum. Attracted to weak signals. Omelets instead. And fresh-squeezed vanity. Success in the isometrics of brunch. Until he threw a coffee cup through my grasping of the situation. The outside wall is reddish brown. There are two closed windows. The upper pane of the left window is cracked. Only a foot or so of each window is visible. Iron bars cover both windows. Each has a window box underneath with lush ivy trailing from it. Under the window on the right the edge of the blue wooden box can be seen. The ivy completely covers the box on the left. Between the two windows are eight squares. Four in a vertical row next to each window. Each square is about eighteen inches tall. There is a three-inch space separating each one. These squares may be merely decorative, but they are at odds with their surroundings. They show the traces of gross neglect. They are painted white, but the paint has peeled off over the years and has left each one with a unique surface, a mismatched set of white and brown compositions. The ones on the left have some unity and continuity as they progress from top to bottom. The patches of brown seem to extend from one square to another. The series on the right is much more haphazard. The brown color is also inconsistent in these four squares. It makes them look more delicate than the ones on the left. Without their context they could easily be mistaken for watercolors. Cruising above cotton puffs of cloud cover. Auburn rays. I was relieved to be far above him. The aftertaste of one of the better airplane meals. He stayed on the ground. Out on the town. A well-filled literary container.

Chicken or beef. Tribal bumps. Two sugared-up kids in the seat behind. Black doves perched on a branch of oak. In cahoots. Pecking at my brain with piercing glee. What's really worth being woken up for? Junk on compact carts. To get away from those dreams? To accomplish these useless things? Invested with so much of me. Of him. I crossed each state on the return trip. Mood always determines the immediate truth. I found him playing marbles to win a queen. And tossed the bones of carrier pigeons over my shoulder. Build a maze with no exit, instead of one with too many. Wooden slats with the sap removed. A handful of postcards to leave myself a trail through his innards. Aroused to fury by waving red rags. Tied to pointy sticks. Fasten your seatbelts in thirteen languages. Nothing is an improvement. Deerskin folded concertina style. The grayed lavender of boiled taro root on seven canvases in his dinky backroom. Playing shuttlecock. A point for each miss. Ostrich meat in a stir-fry. Why the pen name? He didn't know the history of protecting openings. The number of parasites is infinite. Effeminate beings are placed above doorways. Actors. Jesters. Smooth-skinned lads. Flattering mimes. Wearing tinted glass masks. Through the backdoor across a manicured lawn. A satyr-like creature that pulls itself in two. Encouraging the growth of peculiar vegetables. Three clay circles of chipped pottery. Choral specters of fig and peach. Clogged drains that once collected what spewed from open marble mouths. A lone solid rubber sphere. On the central table of a row of thirteen is a crayon drawing. A devil's face. Unkempt orange hair and beard. Aquamarine eyes. Scarlet horns and lips. A startled yet melancholy expression. Golden poppies and common marigolds drawn all around him in an oval border. Objects hold down the edges of the shiny white paper. They form a lazy semi-circle around the drawing. From right to left. A silver spoon. A half-full white coffee cup. A cream pitcher the same color. A black coffee mug with pink pinstripes. Empty. Cheap matching twin tower salt and pepper shakers. Gray plastic. A worn down orange crayon with paper sleeve torn off just above the brand logo. A square aluminum holder with pale blue and yellow artificial sweetener packets. An elbow. Probably of the artist. The drawing had been executed quickly on the paper table cover in the few minutes before the waitress arrived with the food. Linguini and clams. It got on my nerves. The sensitive con. The way he lost things. A book on the subway. His keys in the park at dusk. I rearranged my values as I folded the laundry. The owner's dog panted outside on a short leash. I needed more opinions. Crime novels and long shots. A wet boot on the bathroom floor. An earlier expression of reverence for wilderness lost. Fashionable wildcats butchered nesting fowl. Adorning majestic hats with their nuptial plumes. Pheasants hid in cultivated groves. Tourists flocked to see them on holidays. Acrobats leapt over each other in the midday sun. A playground of trinkets and toys. He couldn't move a muscle. His sore shoulder made it painful to maintain difficult positions. I savored his fragile hesitations. His tender kisses wasted on burnished brass. I kept him in an aviary of orphaned innuendo. Shackled in a leaky gondola. A caged turtledove adrift in an ornamental pond. Spinning water lilies. This was the best it could be for us. He used the internet to look for antique porcelain figures. I studied impatient pompous gestures. He said guys like him were a dime a dozen. Rug burn on his knees and nipples. Bad words and rubber bands. So unschooled and depressed.

A soldier cut from buttered toast. Craving ruthless officials. Hanging gardens over a rickety old fire escape. He painted all his chairs black. A clump of bamboo and one chrysanthemum on the dinette. Theoretically, there's no need for paper, but I like it. A young man is walking down a sidewalk in a dark suit. A briefcase in the left hand and the right in his pant's pocket. Puny leafless trees line the street. The pavement is slick from the last downpour. A large black sedan pulls up along side him and stops. The driver leans over to the passenger side and rolls down the window. Overweight, his moves are clumsy in a snug chauffeur's uniform and cap. The young man comes over to the car and they talk a little. The driver opens the door from the inside and gestures for the young man to join him. He does. The driver pulls the car away from the curb and they continue talking as the car moves along city streets. The young man fidgets with the handle of his briefcase and frowns often. The driver remains upbeat as he tells a story. The young man plays with his fingers and finally puts one hand over the one that holds the briefcase's handle. He taps his index finger as though he's deep in thought. The car stops in front of a large house. The young man gets out of the car and hurries up a stone walkway to the front door. He rings the doorbell. A butler answers the door and ushers him into a wood-paneled vestibule. The young man keeps his suit jacket on, but sets his briefcase down by the door. He's led through a large living room where he waits alone. He studies a large painting of a house in the clearing of a forest. He picks up one framed photograph from a row of ten that are displayed on the mantle above the fireplace. In it, a young man and woman stand on a balcony overlooking the ocean. They are smiling. Their arms are around each other. All of the other photos are portraits of men. He puts the photograph back as an older man in a casual sweater and trousers enters the room. He smiles as they shake hands. He taps the young man on the chest with his index finger and pulls him by the upper arm into the study. Books cover the walls. A porcelain tureen sits on a table set for one. The young man walks over to the table. The older man pats him on the back. The young man looks hungrily at the bowl. He turns and faces the older man. They talk and stare at each other a little while. The older man goes to the table and takes the lid off the tureen. He sets it down and walks over to his desk where he selects a slim cigar from a wooden box. He bites the tip off as he continues talking. He holds the cigar and rolls it with his fingers as he sits down in an overstuffed chair. He runs his finger the length of the cigar and holds it in his lap. He points it at the young man who responds by crossing his arms and leaning back against the edge of the table. Behind him is another large painting. A great eagle flies over a background of snowcapped mountains. The older man stands up and walks back to the desk. He lights the cigar with a heavy metal lighter, takes several puffs to make sure it's well lit. The young man drops into the chair and begins shoveling thick pale soup into his mouth with an enormous spoon. The older man stands near him puffing clouds of smoke. The young man looks up at the older man and smiles. Everyone keeps reinventing the same old songs. A harp-playing ass strutting on hind legs. Descent with modulation. No bedroom door. Brilliant green feathers plucked from the quetzal. I wanted to get him a better birdcage. A month can be a very long time. He walked his starling through the arcades. Balking at gaudy gewgaws. He had a propensity towards derogatory styles. Wild men living on the fringes. He acted out marginal parodies of his struggle to survive. Shooting arrows into the hindquarters of beasts. My apartment made him think of his father. A man cut in two by a window. Pizza crusts under the couch. Sitting in a daze half-dressed for hours. Watching the black and red dragons that crawl up and down the sides of his bamboo pipe. The cup was copper. The mouthpiece jade. After a few bowls he would see them moving. I always caught him when he fell. At least when I was there. A satellite that has lost its bearings. Mildewed archives by the gross. He lit sticks of incense to disguise the carrion stench. My eyes smarted in a cloud of farting anecdotes as I rubbed his sunburned shoulders with a soothing balm. On closer scrutiny it became clear that each page had its own subject. The lack of chin covered by a beard. Its own way of lying. Its own distinct flavor. Why this urge to save everything? I wanted to stay there. With him. Mother-of-pearl. Watching from the other side of the room. I started thinking about my voice. It sounded so different when it came back at me from somewhere else. And there wasn't just one. Or two. Sometimes, when I woke up I was still inside him. Ending tended to be awkward. We took a blanket to the park. Picnic under an oak. Elaborate kites kicking the sky. Jackdaws screaming. Logic unfolding. This self-absorbed study of surfaces never leaves me. He said unnecessary things to me. An elegant formal rigor. I bought him cigarettes and tied him to the wooden chair. Restrained he offered disquieting elements of anonymity. His inability to speak rendered me as a body of water. Not clear, but greenish gray. It could be a lake or a bay. Maybe the slowest part of a river. The water is slightly choppy and reflects bits of sky as blue on its way towards whiteness. In the center five huge logs stick out of the water. They are tied together with a heavy rope in such a way that there must be more logs out of sight behind the five. On top of these logs are two squares of plywood. The square in front is propped up like a sign. White paint has peeled away revealing two thirds of a dark green background. There are two words visible in faded red. They are illegible. The square behind this one is not painted. It is tilted so that half of it is hidden behind the one in front. The grain of the plywood is visible and a few narrow planks have been nailed across it. About fifty feet behind the logs is the base of a bridge anchorage. It's made of immense beige stones assembled like bricks. Some of the stones closest to the water are stained green. He said we are all mirrors and recording devices at the same time. Especially when we are not paying attention to the fact that we are. He didn't like to know what was going to happen next. Surprise was more important than certainty or perfection. He decided against giving me a gilded flicker. Exactly what did happen on that sofa last night? I still picture him there and he says he never was there. Both of us right and wrong to the same degree, but differently. I used to be able to draw pictures of these ideas. Half-frozen fingers would jot down a few words and some wobbly lines. A single idea split into two and those two into four and it continued like that. They split into tolerant and intolerant kinds. I had trouble keeping up with the simple biology. My letters about mathematics bristled with strong language usually reserved for common criminals. He practiced long division punctuated with long distance retorts. At night I visited earlier strata of nightmares. There is comfort in ambivalence. The luxury of being in more that one domain at a time. The intersection of sets. Conclusions became irrelevant to actual exploration. He couldn't understand why I stressed what happens during incubation. I began to watch the shape of light as it hit other shapes. He longed to put me in the big white spaces outside of words. Waiting rooms. Where one thing is always changing into another. I wake up in an old convertible. The top is down. It's mid-morning in the countryside. I am confused, but I have the impression that I swerved off the road to avoid hitting a small dog. I get out of the car and rub my sore neck. I brush some dust off my suit and start walking down the road. I cross over a wooden bridge. Lily pads float on the water underneath it. I come to a tall wire fence and know exactly where to push one of the posts to the side. This action makes an opening just large enough for me to pass through without snagging my suit on the wire. I walk through woods until I reach a huge expanse of pavement. I pass an empty diner that claims to be open twenty-four hours. I continue on and come to a row of identical cube-shaped buildings. I walk inside the first one. It happens to be a bar full of men in tuxedos. They are drinking and carrying on. One is playing an out of tune piano. Another hands me a snifter of brandy. Two guppies swim in a glass bowl on the bar. I feel faint and take a sip of the brandy. One of the men comes over and feels the bump on my forehead. He takes the glass out of my hand and sets it down near the fishbowl. I toss darts with three other men. I ask them if they've seen my friend who was supposed to come here with me. One of them hands me a cigar. Above the dartboard I notice a portrait of two men with their arms around each other. They have enormous mustaches and wear bowties. A few holes from renegade darts have marred their faces. A bald man is very upset about losing the dart game. I reach into my right suit pocket and pull out a handful of birdseed. I go outside and see the dog that caused me to crash my car into the tree. He barks at me and trots off around a corner. I follow him and look at my watch. It has stopped. Now tell it in an order based on recurring colors. He'd accumulated and organized a huge number of photographs that made a network of interrelationships possible I couldn't have imagined otherwise. During breakfast I was misty-eyed. He was afraid of the cut flowers in my room and asked me to guide his exercise regimen. Exchanging rules for regulations. Exuberant somersaults in a cradle of quivering rope. Love flourishes only in impossible situations. He spent the evening changing outfits and rethinking investments. Great views from his rooftop. In the silver cage I eventually bought him he kept a mynah bird that repeated his simpleminded beliefs. A shallow priest with nice things. Jagged scars on the leather-covered scriptures. Relics of battle with higher beings. His tournaments were nostalgic parodies of sodomy and knighthood. Old-time meat recipes written in cursive on index cards. Cheat sheets for fallen angels. I stole some of the most precious things from him. Building blocks in primary colors. Fake designer purses and shoes. A straw basket full of strawberries and little hurts. We never got the ritual of domestic bliss. Only bonding before surgery in a hospital that broadcasts prayers at ungodly hours. Camouflaged speakers at the head of every bed. Just like this one. Shit had its proper place back then. It used to run down the center of avenues and boulevards. Now it's just branded on the sidelines. Even empty space is saturated with traditional implications. He had another subway mishap. People thought everything in his studio was an art object. Spinach flan and leek puree. I passed the stone without pain. Randomly interspersed images were followed by an extended sequence of the same images in the exact same order. Not anything to do with color this time. After a while no other sequence looks right. Transparent sheets of red hang in front of my eyes. An excellent cabernet. Some more time alone. A conversation between components overlapping in my thoughts. He said I was imposing. Snapshots of someone else's holiday projected on top of each other. A condensation of generic viewing habits. He left a pile of things on the bed that wouldn't fit in his suitcase. A shirt. Two pairs of underwear. Unwashed. A half bottle of vitamins. A loaf of homemade bread. Stupid reasons. Pristine absolutes. Why do I have to gather up all these little pieces? He tucked his goodbyes inside boneheaded magazines. What a relief. Drain and cut lengthwise through the center membrane. Garnish with stuffed green olives. Punk rock softly in the lounge. Venetian blinds half-closed. He lurked at cop conventions and snuck into theaters after the movies started. A hat. Eggs. A crow's claw. A tube of glue. Everything shot from above. He liked middles best. I sleep in snatches here and there. Television sound in the next room. So many things are expensive and not incredible. The bed had a lump running the length of it. His wife's car idling in the driveway. Dreadful halftime show. Fat lizard in a polyester affair. Subdued and soft in the video glow. Not swishy. Pixel images that spoke directly to gladiatorial identities. Clutter and clarity coexist in a riot of color. Bright red fiberglass above the crunching of rubber on gravel. A talisman for a kind of shrewdness in business matters. A disgusting creature from the dark remainders of ancient fireside tales.

Have another beer. A thick kiss on my navel. I feel woozy from the new capsules, but the symptoms are fading. One by one. Whitened bones were placed around the entrance to our burrow. Each new actual or imagined position allowed for new relationships to occur between the others. I filled small stone cups of rice vinegar to the brim. We sprinkled our bloody tongues with notions of mescaline and dressed each other in the skins from the animal herds outside the city. He became a riddle plundered by elliptical references. A face of transparent laminate. I recorded the fractal smears of his ceaseless movement. The best moments built on dualities. He told me he had never been able to achieve a painterly surface in his mind and later fell asleep with my fingers deep in his throat. Two young men sit facing each other on a narrow cobblestone street. They flip a gold coin back and forth between them. One of them is exasperated because the other drops the coin almost every time it is flipped to him. An older man strolls up to them spinning his hooked cane. He points it at them, but immediately turns to face a third young man who is standing near the entrance to a shop. This youth waves a circular woven fan. The older man speaks and smiles at him revealing his perfect straight teeth. The younger man looks away as if bored. The older man turns his back on the younger man and places a cigarette in his mouth. A young woman shouts down to him from a window on the second floor across the street. The exasperated coin flipper stands up and lights the older man's cigarette. They walk together down curving stone steps past a fruit stand. They stroll a bit farther and stop at the next stand to nibble some baked bread. The vendor doesn't ask the older man to pay. The younger man follows the older man through an arched doorway. The door shuts once they've passed through. In a recessed courtyard I caught a glimpse. I peered between the branches and leaves that shielded them from predators and photographers. One cardinal gingerly placing seeds inside another's open beak. At the base of the old oak tree was a black box with two black knobs. It emitted a series of clicks, whirrs, and buzzes that perplexed me. I was intrigued by this mysterious apparatus. I hoped it might be preserving a link in the long chain of lost musical traditions. To pretend you know when you don't know is a bad way to begin. This is called the dimmed light. His rebellion was merely the urge to be different. But that made him part of the group that wants to recognized as individuals. The jack-of-all-trades takes too much time. They push draped bodies on carts past my door at night. The universe hidden in itself. There is no escape. Death is just homecoming. A silly little thing in the scheme of big things. I am a foreigner as long as I breathe the outside air in and send it out again changed. There are days when I admire anyone who gets anything done. Some weep over a banquet that never was. Out of sight. Dozens of dragonflies feasted on insects too small for me to detect. My body is at odds with the person I am becoming. Animosity grows in abandoned cavities. The process feeds on itself. A mismatch. Inevitable. Why was there a sense of shock at particular intervals? I wanted to insert octaves at the timid junctures of his melodies. The wrong blend leads to disaster. Fatal black lumps exchanging signals. He had to get rid of his birds. And find someone to snuggle up to for tenderness. Depending on dye to achieve the right effect. I tied all kinds of words together into a pulsating web of ideas that were difficult to unravel. I shunned the bloated oracle that convinces most people to take its simple ideas as their own revelation. He had a knack for pinpointing basic feelings and making them larger than they are. I liked to travel along the edge of that sphere. Reshuffling my heritage. Getting stuck in snug holes. The gritty stuff. I rewrote his old novels. Carved up the time. Down in there. Digging around. Reordering the layers. He was afraid he would choke and I wouldn't notice. I promised him an elaborate funeral. The clash in perspective between one language and another. A cock fight. No fossil record. No curios on a stick. Just a slight residual limp. Ever ready for his close-up. Choir of angles. Calling for back up. Sine and cosigner. Heavy-duty sleeping pills. Wildcat piss and petrified snake tongues rained down from the sky. Obscuring the calculated tumble of a harlequin quail. Kiwi fruit and acorns. I couldn't write it down the way he told me. He used a blackboard. The same figures in colored chalk as before. An aversion to writing letters made them look like postcards. I didn't have to sit on the edge of my seat. I didn't want to predict the result. He was no longer anxious about what he was doing. Sobriety made him subtle. He went on and on without regard for where he took himself. A forest is always moving. I felt a tug towards finance. Glaciers cleared the way. Though what I cared about most had nothing to do with earthly riches. A box of slugs turns into loathsome soup as the survivors feed on the corpses of the others. He didn't notice inconsistency. Perhaps he lacked an affinity for target values. What happens when a single note is held for the duration of a lifetime? It was like porno that you actually wanted to see again. We split the bill. No miracle required. His progressive streak was wonderful in translation. Another sprinkling of seeds. Minute discriminations undermined each reading. Superceding commonplace cadences and random remarks about nature. I contemplated restlessness into the wee hours of predawn. Half-talking. Half-singing a private lexicon of sighs, gasps, groans, screams, and rattles. He asked me to experiment on him. To make him the object of my scorn. I marveled at the clarity of such youthful cravings. His inability to censor his own thoughts. Each kink sure of its own cultivation. Overgrown blades of grass to be mowed down and trimmed into a momentary lawn at the jungle's edge. He dripped over sticky situations. Pissing me off. Lapping up displeasure in the face of scientific abuses. He sniffed out the dank corners of personalities that needed to dominate unfairly. Laughing at poetry that made its way to the page. We plunged into chill shadows. Imitating nationalistic disasters in metaphysical ruts of demolition. Sweaty shivers in the first draft of harsh winter. Inexperience has little use for the replay of the seasonal. Its circles are lopsided. The lines warped. Refusing to rhyme. Those wonderful brown fogs come creeping down the streets. Blurring lights and changing houses into monstrous shapes. He did a great deal of sobbing and shoe smelling. All the online research in the world hadn't prepared him for lucid fury. And even less for the eventual sluggishness of unexamined responses. Aimless days decorating a corrugated box. A hint of pathos in a bush warbler's cry. Severe and sparkling spittle butts up against the languid pangs of buggery. Sometimes missing the whole idea. One half prick. One half cunt. His body chiseled against the ground. A scrap of towel. A pink mule. Flocks of tiny geese through evening smoke. Morning glory desperate for sunshine. Clutching pillows in deepest slumber. He looked so fragile, but I broke, too. The radiators going full blast. Hectic wasted forms. Elephant impressions. Soggy chalk drawings wavered. Pitting spring against autumn. How many years left? Honeysuckle trailing over a wicker fence. Wistful charms. Squeezing out booklets that betray contempt for the consumer. Later on. A lamb and a monkey, too. Some sweet potato pie. He suggested the photographs I took bore no relation to true literature. My parents used to burn them in the fireplace. Back then he lived in an old cupboard under the stairs. Its slanting ceiling was painted dark blue. Silver foil stars reflected the soft candlelight. He avoided short ordinary words. Bacon sandwiches at midnight. Everything in town was closed except for one movie theater. A lake with enormous lily pads. A small dog races along into a field with horses and darts out into a country rode in front of my car. I swerve and run off the road into a tree. I wake up and stumble out of the car. One of the front wheels is still spinning an inch above the ground. My young friend is in the backseat. His feet are propped up on the front seat. He jumps out of the car and we both take a few minutes to survey the damage. He changes his dress shoes for tennis shoes and we begin walking down the road. We come to a bridge that crosses the lake. My friend springs up onto a brick barrier to walk arms outstretched along the top of it. On the other side of the bridge he jumps down and we walk together into a thick wooded area. We come to a tall wire fence and move along it a ways. He pushes on one of the fence posts and it leans to the side making an opening in the wire just wide enough for us to slip through. We come to a clearing paved with concrete. We pass a blank white sign nailed to a post and an abandoned moving van with checkerboard designs on the sides. Finally, we reach a row of makeshift houses. We enter the first one. The front door is ajar. No one is inside. It's decorated for a party. A player piano tinkles an old drinking song. I ladle some red liquid from a crystal punch-bowl into two matching cups. We clink them together before drinking and set them down with the other half-empty cups around the bowl. I pick up a still smoking cigar from an ash-tray. He taps on the side of a fishbowl. Two guppies float belly up. We look into the kitchen. A half-frosted cake sits on a heavy oak table. Several loaves of baked bread cool on a metal rack. We go back outside. I find a container of yogurt squished on the pavement and a stack of full milk bottles in metal crates. We walk over to a minivan that's parked nearby. My friend finds an albatross lying by one of the wheels. He picks it up and cradles it. It's unconscious. He sets it down under the hedge that lines the lawn. We go through a side door into the garage. The door slams shut and we are mo-mentary blind in the darkness. It's not quite the same story when he tells it. Without light we lost track of each other. He admitted he was taking sleeping pills every night. Classic work long suppressed was openly sold. Irritating gaps and lags healed. I had trouble getting much down. Odd mo-ments. The travel urge. He stood perched over my desk. Try-ing to read words that weren't on the page yet. He heard water dripping in the tub whenever he was still. Everything I wrote was written by a person he hadn't met. I sulked at his ruthless morality. His extreme reactions. Maybe he just wanted more attention than he could accept. Stress is in-creased through the use of the imperative voice. Plum blos-soms on the back of his mirror. A storehouse of contaminat-ing scents. He never lived in a territory that defined itself. In a constantly shifting environment it's much easier to migrate than to evolve. He searched for underlying themes in a new string of anecdotes. The frailty of morning dew on a shepherd's purse. Timid twigs at twilight. He clutched the gray hair clippings of his dead grandmother in his fist. At first he would do nothing more than kiss. Each particle has to have its own distinctive material. I was fixated on a cartoon. The continents drift apart like slow ships. Cooling brothers. Our liquid cores congealed into young rocks. Finding the dark under leafy trees. Crickets. Rows and rows inside a factory. Robots or rice pudding in plastic cups. I started telling him other people's stories. His watch ticking under the bed after he'd gone. The land itself bears evidence of its journeys. Parking spaces. The surrounding context. Jangling spurs in a station wagon. Transcribing the hidden things. Flesh to paper. Secret fuel. Pungent white radish. Beyond reach. The pale cries of ducks on darkening waters. The friction of reminders. He liked that idea of being bound by the dead. Lengths of cotton rope that held others before him. Crafty rascals. Sneaking puppies. He said people in therapy became so self-centered they stopped doing fun things. The history of guts is not much different than the history of islands. Best friends detesting each other. Canaries picking fortunes out of a pile. He bought his mother a dishwasher. She bought him a grave next to her church. Snap dragons. I thought my thoughts were better than his. A sallow ocean full of sea scorpions. Courage that comes from a bottle. For the sake of cargo. Jolly sharks. I preferred gambling to shoplifting. Irregular exchanges between worlds. Butterflies hung in the air for a few seconds. Smalltime operators. Persons of some standing that would gather in the spreading darkness. They lived on nectar and specialized in their own sweet flowers. Some of the greatest birds are flightless. I had too much black tea. It felt good to crank something out in a few hours. I killed dozens of them before finding the right character. The projectionist burned the film and everyone started talking. Numbskulls and nitwits. Slit ears and noses. Inconsolable. A collection of the most common colors. Subsisting on silk and weeds. Hauling mattresses. The shallow sounds along the coast provided safe asylum. He locked me in the library by accident. I kissed holes in his books. He swore at newscasters through the screens. Little animals out of folded squares. By repeating myself do I make it better or worse? Sometimes the best thing is to just ignore them. Yet I find myself counting again. Floating bodies. One thing moves into another. The nothingness of a black dot.

ETCETERAS OR AN EPITOME OF RUINS

And I continue rubbing as though into an emptiness, as though the pressure of the fingers pressed against nothingness.

Robert Morris —*Blind Time Drawings*

…in a little while others will find their past in you…

Walt Whitman —*Leaves of Grass*

The reader always starts at an end that begins. It's time to admit I don't know the whole story. It gets hard to balance the negative slant. Something had to go. The toxins. The gently sloping derangements of the years. These little scraps are supposed to preserve something. My intentions? Awkward placebos. Some of them had moustaches. Puffy faces. Mushy heads. Unreliable eyes. It already went. Brown bottle in my hand. Thick purple suspenders. Denim pulled tight between. Slipping back into the shadow of an old routine. The details ran away. All kinds of feelings bump into each other. I had to learn how to empty my shelves. A betrayal in fact. Just a smidgen. Simply decorated promises. I keep looking at people. Such slow movements. A complex pattern of stains in an empty theater. Dirty sneakers. Traveling hands. I smelled the smell of my childhood. The skinny staircase. Honey and vinegar. Angel food cake. Yellowed photographs under cracked glass. Peeled apples browning in a bowl by the rocking chairs. Authors on cards in a tin box. Mint fondle. No drawers. Slick warm breeze. Hand-cranked playground. A pan of melted butter. New ways to think about holes. A rent stabilized aggression. Where the living room carpet ended and the kitchen tiles began. The abrupt line disappears.

The view was ever shifting after panoramic windows were installed. The setting sunlight on storm clouds never reveals their sharp tragic cores. He claimed there was a subversive way of singing songs. But his references didn't arrive from the depths. He left no room for unique objects. How easy it is to lie to everyone. Over and over. The emaciated economy of line and color. Tossing lobsters into boiling water. For sport. The shell of the person that was. Exquisite gold-tinged surfaces. More gibberish or one of the ten phrases. Joyous in another world. There was nothing at all in it for me. That is to say. The void appears even in the formulaic.

If you disagree, disagree in such a way that it makes a better story. The grid maintains more than regularity. My mind does not work like a computer. Why do they keep saying that? It is here where everything seems to flow that opposed ideas clash in silence. I long for eyes that can see what language does to me. Each language that disappears makes the world a narrower place. But perhaps I don't how to recognize the one that comes to takes its place. How does a picture come from a thousand words? Who uses categories for what ends? I will be pegged again. Look, instead, for something that doesn't exist. People find what they're looking for.

Through a pair of binoculars. The infinite variableness of the ideal tree.

A pillow over the face makes a night. It feels like the wrong things are visible. Attention settles on convenient surfaces. The past is an embedded future. It's time for a rewrite. Animated bouncing microbes from old science films projected onto the flag. One note from an electric guitar. Ferocious humping at every beach and rest stop along the way. Odd combo. Soft belly. Needy fingers. No poetry there. Nibbling stalks of celery. Antique silver pillbox wedged under an elastic waistband. Crick in the neck. Finding new kilter.

Steel pellets hit the window near the table I write this on. Someone is tapping on a computer keyboard in the next room. I'm using a pencil worn down to the wood. These sounds should be mixed better. All the time I've spent writing this book I have returned to this one specific incident. It's not in my journal. I sat on the toilet. There were cacti in pots on the window ledge. I looked outside at the flat roof of the garage two houses away. It caved in as I stared. It made a loud unfamiliar crash that split my thoughts into two parts. The part that knew it had happened and the part that couldn't yet believe it had.

A batch of brownies. A train conductor left his watch under my bed. Scared ostrich. Enormous zoom lens in a gym bag. Black as burnt biscuits. Piece of dad. Musty cigar tip spittled with hazelnut tones. Little crowd of admirers. That cozy pile. Caffeine jangling him under all that green. The difference between childish and child-like. A nation of elderly men fluent in baby talk. The bulk of it written in cursive on the blackboard. Punishment doesn't have to be a kind of revenge. I found myself pulsing deep inside a jaguar, a young girl, a handful of mythological creatures I couldn't name, and some of the old men. Sometimes they changed me into complementary forms. The spell of stunned dendrites. My switchboard reconfigured. I veered toward the mathematical. Everything crammed onto fifty note cards. Forty-five dollars for the cab. Three tiny scars behind his ear. His scalded hand had healed. Someone else could probably write about him as a person to admire. An exceptional person. I could only see the selfish edge of the bluish aura surrounding him. Hair drooping in his eyes. Constrictive scaffolding that has more substance than the building behind it. Any reconstruction of him is less than fiction. Hatred brought me closer to him than I had been to anyone else. The mark of the twins on his thigh.

They speak to me through microphones. It's convenient for them to be smug as they try to eradicate bewitchment from language. I only like them when I'm lonely. After a very long silence. I never agreed to this distancing, but I don't know what I would do if it were gone. That abyss is where home ought to be. An electric clarity wrests me out of entrenched patterns. The fear and comfort of a movement toward eclectic behavior. Toward seclusion. Always the voices come and make of me a mirror or medium for every figure that rushes through my mind. I try to alter them physically or at least by capturing images on paper. It's a kind of love I don't think I can have. I don't know how to say important things on my own. It takes on aspects of prostitution. I think I'm paying for surrogates.

Outside the room was a huge clock on the side of another building. It lit up at dusk every evening. A little later each day. He told me I couldn't lose. He didn't see the competition. In here, it's both of us at once. Parts of both. And then everybody else. His questions formed my own magnifying glass. I went out to the corner store. The air carried the scent of basketball. I brought back cigarettes and we smoked.

My left hand started tingling from all the typing. Flickering body parts made of light moved back and forth in a furious blur. His wet skin was the color of the corkboard on my wall. I pinned photographs of men to it. Cut carefully from magazines. Two days of heavy rain. Floorboards were warping. Water dropped into a metal bucket as the crack in the ceiling became longer and wider. I put down pots and pans to catch the copper liquid from new leaks. Plaster peeled and hung down at the crack's edge. I finally used a staple gun to attach a plastic drop cloth to the ceiling. It funneled every drop into the sink. I began to welcome the smell of mildew and rotting wood.

Slow waltzes. Half spoken. Half sung. A soft cloud of non-specific sadness that only disperses when he laughs then collects itself afterward. He liked the kind of boys who can't decide whether to study hard or just rub their crotches and shift around in their café chairs. He could push a book into people's homes as if it were a can of floor wax. Women lined up to have his name spelled out for them. I wondered how he could keep from shooting with all the stimulation. It was the perfect number of mouths for total service. Such small portals for viewing. Reading the entries in reverse order. Eating the marrow out of bones. Slim pickings. I didn't have to learn to embarrass myself. I put my hand around its girth and squeezed. The whole thing pushed its way into the room with me. In the dim red light I couldn't tell what color it was. A finely controlled instrument nonetheless. And during the most dramatic part of the best song a cell phone started ringing. He had a voice that could open a door and scrape the paint off it at the same time.

He was waiting there for me to return. And in that quiet interval he invented a whole way of writing that everyone else ignored. He didn't notice its desperate halitosis. Its tubercular organ drones. My feet sank into thick foam padding covered with vinyl. I backed off and heard him whisper something less than flowery. He started spouting headlines like fishhooks. They swam around me in possessive circles. He was flabbergasted when I placed my hands on both sides of the hole and bobbed up and down like an epileptic. How can a cradle be so formidable? It's the way my mind approached the world. I kept it all in my throat.

Work is a slap in the face. I'm accustomed. How to establish vacation autonomy at the office. A bad year for viruses. More dressing in silence. The light nutty flavor of his ejaculate on my tongue so long afterwards. A fear of being in debt. I hope to find some real gems. The all-night donut shop across town. Injecting custard into soft replicas. Many introspective days in a row. The good sleeping nights are gone. I'm wavering. Another artist who will never be satisfied. Sporadically productive. Second fiddle. Skidding through a third rate porn flick for the third time. The newness wears off and over time I don't hear the soft music piped in over the sound system.

Who decides universality anyway? The same motion repeated over and over dulls the mind.

I began to notice where borders existed between me and other people. And when they were trespassed. The secure self is an illusion. Things get inside. And things get out. What stays? I learned to stop gagging. Everything in its proper place. Ideas are more important than objects. But wait. I like sweeping passages of intense loveliness. Jagged fringes. Relentless fires in tidy neighborhoods. Making room for the cold bluish light of complex formulas. As long as it's a couple of doors down. The young tire so easily of pushy older men. All lavender and violet. Munching frilly squares on silver trays. Not my cup of tea. The tedium of politics in large buildings where filtered sunlight illuminates the hard surfaces of every wall and appliance. What good are record collections and pencil sharpeners? What is this huge vacancy? Cleverness gets too close. I've misspelled plagiarism so many times.

There were more rainy days. On the first sunny one an old man was on the roof next door. I could smell the molten tar in the big paint bucket as he covered plywood boards with tarpaper. He slopped the hot tar on top and spread it around with a hoe. The garden below was in full bloom. My flower boxes were bursting with miniature pink and pale orange roses. I sat by the open windows a long time staring. He surprised me with a wet kiss. His leather fingers cradling my chin firmly so I couldn't turn away. Tongue undulating. A secret jellyfish in the darkest deep waters. The bittersweet smoke taste merged with the smell of his glove. I pulled sideways to break the kiss and scraped my cheek on his prickly stubble. He won't talk to me and look at me at the same time. I don't like his baggy pants. He sells a shampoo made with mud from the sea. Full of salt. A violent film is on the monitor above the sink. I look forward to the hot shaving cream he will dab next to my ears when he's done. It seems to me the aliens that take over the humans have already won. It soothes me. His razor doesn't sting. The only blood that runs is made of pixels from his screen. But always tiny pieces of dread just before the first snip. Something about every haircut makes it the first one.

An excerpt of hot air. Breathtaking and affordable. He takes credit cards. Behind a yellow light source. It protects the eyes from the parade of privileged traits. A flawed child against the background of his own adulthood. Who can trace the history of an emotion? Something disappears into the future. A last encounter with a soldier. Wreaking havoc with the trashy boyfriend. Two-pronged losses. Easily swayed, yet not wanting it. The jagged fringe mistaken for a halo. Out of focus mementos from his maiden voyage. A sprinkling of opium. The disparity during travel between what is expected and what is experienced. It won't be novel next time. Next to nothing. Everything is colored by movement. Even the space between words.

Between mother's cookies and father's rocking chair. Her sewing machine and the house he designed. I cut out pieces of construction paper, scribbled on them, and glued them to a piece of cardboard. A simple comfort. No risk. No pressure. No deadline. What is lost in the search for ways to known and unknown readers?

Sentences that trail off at the end. I go over them with a red magic marker. Tracing the lines of complex emotions as they fly through the air. Snail trails for a ghost town. A tingling crept up my arms and across my chest as I walked through immaculate vacant rooms. I felt like peeing in the bathwater or arguing with a shrill housewife over tea and furniture. The windowpanes had no streaks. Only the hint of bleach and porcelain coming from the bathroom. Dust remover makes absolutely no sense. I feel the tug of time. The urge to be emptied of everything is more attractive than I want to admit.

Next to nothing. Infantile lovers with omniscient smiles. Tongues that taste of whisky or gin. That was right up my alley. A row of mats spread out on the floor. Stick to the business at hand. Airport phones distorting voices into nonsense syllables. The glistening background was made from old subway station tiles. Buckets of plastic orbs full of lubricant. I luxuriated in someone else's disaster. The ineptitude of drunken handymen ushered in a new era of solitude. Melting snow left dark holes whose patterns I couldn't fathom. It wasn't so long ago that no one had a computer at home. They were the size of small houses and held within them a symphony of brilliant secrets. So many still believe a bearded old man sits up there in the clouds watching us and jabbing us with ridiculous intrusions. I spent a long time marking up a copy to demarcate pauses, stresses, and changes of mood. I should have invited more people. It's so difficult to feign confidence.

I began to make my own books. I made the paper and wrote the words. I collated the pages and bound them together. A limited edition of thoughts. Everything in order to make it my own. But did I succeed in making something that was mine?

Cities in boxes. I walk by them every day on the way to work. They don't dwarf me any more. I am taller than they are sometimes. Grandeur. Majesty. Imposition. Shiny. Steel and glass. You never leave them. Even in the countryside I see myself inside them. Or are they inside me? Books full of other lives that move through the soft tissues I call me. Rebuilding them in the deserts and forests of inner continents.

The audience wasn't large. A cluster of precious peccadilloes. Bar veterans. Merging together in odd configurations that are lost when I reread them out loud. It's unclear if anyone ends things. Gentle rocking motions. I bit my own tongue in search of feminine qualities. A mind in the grip of vengeance has sharper teeth. A wad of severance pay and a couple of plane tickets. Not much writing reflects the way I think. It doesn't jump around enough. I was thrown off by the use of miracles instead of murderers. Most ideas remain partially formed. Particles lost in a big house in a row of big houses surrounded by rows of other big houses.

I found fully dressed serenity in folded wet laundry. Lulled to sleep by a series of convincing conclusions. Unseasonably warm. Hot ash. Hospital regimen. The glowing tip. The numbers game. Too many different trains. Punk rock rattled tinny speakers. Double whammy. Blushes when you call him names. I chose to stay on this side of the epiphany. So in most people's books, I guess I'm not the main character. I couldn't help it. I just saw him coming towards me, all shiny and formless. I threw my head back. Blinking. Coughing. I saw a half-eaten sandwich on the table. Something smoldering in the ash try. I felt the dirty linoleum on my bare feet.

But I refused to lose control of myself. I don't care if it ruins the story. I don't care if I'm not racing towards somebody's predestined moral. I approach and back away again and again. Leaving him there. Twitching. Struggling. The look on his face like a fluffy pillow.

Skuzzy little bugger. Had never read an entire book. His words rushed passed me. A barren landscape outside a train window. Except for hundreds of spindly trees whose blurring branches seemed to reach inside and scrape the sadness and anger away. The calm blessing of a useless stupor. A whole life tied together with hot pink nylon twine. No give. No glory. Scissors stay out of reach. Air conditioning is important on nights like these. Gorging himself on simple rhythms. An old wooden horse left out by the garbage cans.

Cops ate donuts in that chair. I tied objects to it over and over again thinking I could transmit something to them. My thoughts in the shape of fingertips. Pointed needles. I sat there, too. Reading their favorite books in that same chair. I tethered the words to my flesh. There was no resistance. Time takes it away. Lazy boy. Feet up. Head back. Eyes closed. Lips parted. We shouldn't lct mctaphors mean what we make them mean. We don't even try to stop meaning them. Lazy boy. You're a foreigner in your own country. What do you want?

He walked in shoes made of their skin. I rode one at my uncle's farm when I was ten. I drank the pale milk extracted from them by machines in cramped quarters. Cows are content in children's books. They come with bells around their necks. Chewing grass all day. Walking slowly through funny scenes in old movies. I watched him prepare them for their injections. They looked more and more cadaver-like. Bluish limp creatures at his feet. I held him in front of me by his bony shoulders. A flaking gray diamond sagging against me. On the oil-stained carpet he'd left his scuffed-up shoes. One black, one brown. Similar, but not the same style. I saw pink flesh through the holes in the bottom of his socks. He used to be a quiet pinball ace. He clutched a shoebox full of broken seashells and said they were the only artifacts of his waning interest in evolution. I kept the grains of sand he left on the carpet. I invented a new name to fit my mood. Looking fishy and fearful. An essaying walk. Pretty much finished with television. Wanting to be begged for something. Anything at all. Yes, I'm streamlining everything. Fuck me into a blathering word ambrosia. Or so he said as I instructed him in the fine art of keeping my phrases wet. To love the taste of dust on the tongue. Snapshots to prove it. Smart as a whip. Shits fire. Macho sawdust and a muster of peacocks. Going to get my license renewed.

Desperate for decency. I strive to organize my financial well-being instead of catering to toothless vampires. I still long for the complexity of the classics. Stumbling into a cave painted with ancient drawings of animals and their hunters. Hands so large mine disappeared when he grasped them. I felt the tug of gentle concern. He liked to arrange things into categories according to a system no one else could decipher. Rows and rows of colors designated for specific body parts. Hands so large they seemed built for playing the sweeping intricacies of cloying atmospheres. It smelled like someone lived there. Someone tired of complaining about life in such a little room. The bare rudiments of the same old plot. A museum of cosmetics. Soft confections. Surrounded by metal. Six-sided fibs. I collected these little tins caring nothing about the sweetness inside. Even the tinted plastic squares held in order on a silver chain. The packaging lies. The odors of every big city. The sound of a lid snapping into place. Closed for renovations.

Over time. Heat had warped the oven door. Hot air escaped into the kitchen. The black knobs were from another stove. I burned everything. Baking was impossible. When the radiators didn't work, I turned the oven on with the door open. The pilot light went out and when I tried to light it the gas had built up. A burst of flame singed my eyebrows and lashes. It was part of a poster. Something I found hard to throw away. A printed photograph somehow has more value than a digital image. Spirits that still roam the earth. I like saving mistakes. Overexposed. Fuzzy. Badly cropped. Mother always managed to cut father's head off in the pictures. Just the nice white pressed shirt from the neck down. Everyone's eyes are closed. A fat thumb breaks the frame. A young boy stranded in the desert. The second best were stuck loose in the back of the album so they fell out whenever someone pulled it off the shelf. Sad little boys lamenting the past. Scattered on the floor. They want a phone call once a year. Quick-setting cement. Ambivalent appeasements for tawdry affairs. If they let anything into the empty core, they will be defined.

There's much less this time. Does that make it feel true to life? Was he believable? Or even better. Was he reproducible?

I let my hair grow out. Part of a circuitous route. Café to café. In safari clothing. No gold medal. No longer speaking. Thick smoke over acoustic guitar. A table made out of an unfinished wooden door. Lines and lines of writing underneath shot off in all directions. I couldn't make sense of the words after I read them. All meaning just slipped away. I found him lying downstairs by the entrance. Eyes wide. Lying in a pool of personas. He had just finished his breakfast. There were mysterious scribbles on his notepad. Something must have ruptured. I considered his agony. One side of the record seemed to last for hours. Pancreas or spleen. Reflective surfaces still find the sadist who only wept through other men's tears. Both of us are moving in lubricated silence toward simultaneous translation.

It's tempting to stay adrift in all this. Lots and lots of typos. And urgency. I can always tell when I'm tired. Where is the back of my mind? It's a matter of preparation. Allowing the silly questions until a good one comes along. I would sit in the corner of the room. Right over there on the floor. In the dust bunnies. An enormous insect crawls right through my text. I back away from it while studying the short even strokes that make it creep through my words. Passed the rapture. Up walls to places I can never reach. How far does it go? There is no headless beauty. I read that in a toilet. Watching the skeletal mechanism of our convenient living situation winding down. Plenty of gods stuffed in pockets. They sell drugs to most of their customers. The cops shut them down sooner or later. Without ceremony and a generous glob of spittle. Cheap brand names. Glass bottles with poison inside. Each one a different color. Blue sugared water at every meal. All belongings packed in boxes. Cardboard boxes stacked in the center of the living room. For months I walked around them. Years lopped off the last part of my life. I grip our serrated daily bread knife in my hand. It's harder and harder to stay inside and easier to want to stay there.

Always talking about the weather. There were guards in the tombs. The dead become jars of powder. The spoken parts were dreadful. Tiny pictures in a series make a language or a gesture on stone walls. That ghost ahead of schedule. A kind of writing that remembers moments I would forget. Divvies them out on lousy postcards. A sentence or a touch that changes the trajectory of a thought. Interrupts the disconnection of numbers. Fumbling with clothes. Maybe it's better to not give someone what they need. A nibbled ear. The bonus check. A lovely treat. Licking salt off a neck. The paper cup full of pills. Another inch. The chance to get away unscathed. The phone call. The disabling guilt. Dozens of books. Another phone call. The traffic noise. The whole sonata. Solid technique. A sore quivering hole. The advantage of experience. Exhibitions. Films. Parties. And always more talking about the weather.

Anyway, I miss you. You showed me the backside of nightlife. Your lunacy carved its warped shapes exactly into my brain. You sent mute specters determined to rattle the cupboards. By now, my little wormhole, you don't exist outside of these pages. And soon, neither will I.

There appear to be too many sides to the story. My mind has become a battlefield. Reason could just slip away anytime. Eternity in the dark place. Who said day and night are the same thing? Not the same one who said diaries are the lowest form of writing. I was lost in the gray areas awhile. Slutty literary habits. There are kinds of thinking that aren't allowed in well-lit locations. I abandoned prudish thumbnail sketches. Too much wine with dinner. I gouged craters in the plastic seat cover of his new car with a broken pencil. He was not shy about touching. Someone's childhood wrapped in a fluffy towel. Sturdy legs poking out. Burnt taste buds. I could use better diagrams.

I took them from restaurants and bars. Ephemeral souvenirs that went up in flames before they could become nostalgia. Boxes of them or books. Wood or paper. Some flared up in the dark when struck. The brightly colored tips of others would crumble, sometimes five or six times in a row before one would light. I could use them to light my candles and burn incense. Or to disguise a stinky fart. But mostly, without a fireplace or a smoking habit, I just lit them to watch them burn.

We never resolve anything. There's only the shaking of hands. Obscene fish jumping out of the ocean with mouths gasping. Some were splashing in the shallow water or lying on the sand. I sensed the rumblings of discontent as I sorted through crumpled clothes in banged-up cardboard boxes. A little death is good for bringing back the intensity. Fuel for progress. Real or imagined. It exudes a kind of cantankerous charm in older people. A funnel for rage. My character walks away from the afternoon and nothing happens. Everything rattling around him. A wall of glass shatters. All is radiant white. Paintings are hung across from each other in the living room. Music scores stacked under chairs. It is the accumulation of things. Odd clues. Breaking someone's rules. More case studies. Hosting unpleasant scenes. Coffee and sarcasm. Mocha body with a black stripe down the center. A row of tiny legs on each side. Pinned to a piece of black cardboard. The reward for being special.

Apologies make a person feel clean so they can enjoy getting dirty all over again. Abacus or rosary? I never had another piano lesson. The curtains stayed up long after he moved away. Thankfully. We can always talk about structure and underlying philosophies. It's nice to know that seeing clearly doesn't make it feel better. Fear of hell creeps back in dreams. Does evil come from inside people or is it a judgment? It's the same with beauty or yelling out the window at the neighbors. Encounters are rewarding, but maybe not in the way we expect them to be. There was a plague of messiahs. Brightly colored human forms. Sunny skies. Puffy clouds. And tables heaped with food. I swallowed a full bottle of tranquillizers. Washed them down with vodka. Threw them up a few minutes later and did some finger paintings. I tacked them up all around me in the kitchen. They looked like whirlwinds.

Another dream where architecture is more important than people. I made drawings of every house so I could remember them when I woke up. Each one was unique. They had more sides than a cube. The air was clean and crisp. I wasn't sure if this was a vacation spot or home. Residents were disposable props. Inert experiments finally rubbing up against new elements. I might have been a pillow. But I couldn't agree to meet them in the afterlife. Every aspect was mapped out. Gorgeous colors ripped through damaged speakers into the darkness. Above the audience's heads. They made a very long line and paid to have things they didn't understand projected through them. Weren't there days when entertainment wasn't only for the passive? Maybe it's okay to look at the sun on television. Even blobs have their shining moments. Wage earners can be just as fucked-up as panhandlers. As long as they can pay rent someone will put up with their stupidity for a very long time.

Knife or lullaby. There is no return to an unambiguous perspective. Some people need crowds so they can listen to themselves. Beds can be shops. A book loved can disappear. Bloodshot eyes sparkle with hope in a genius of average intelligence. Again the problem with approximation. The backseat driver finds museums a bit brutal. They say it's time to lighten up. But I seem to be running out of commentary. I've had it both ways and I want to see the world for the first time. It's a fine collection. Rows of huge pictures hung on such small hooks. I am drawn to the space between each pair of them. The light from two spotlights overlaps and makes a parenthetical oval between their frames.

ACKNOWLEDGEMENTS

The following is an attempt to chronologically list many who, on the long zigzagging pathway towards this book, have contributed to its unfolding—through conversation, through kindness and encouragement, or by living life in some way that has inspired me (in some cases all three):

Doris Marliave, Curt Thomas, Janis Lipzin, Beatrice Mallek, Ellen Zweig, Robert Bell, Leslie Thornton, Nanos Valaoritis, David Rosenboom, Maggie Payne, Thomas Zummer, Samuel Delany, Evan Senreich, Bill Brent, Jim Gladstone, David Rosen, Paul Willis, Patrick Califia, Marilyn Jaye Lewis, Mikael Karlsson, Jessica Treat, Richard Labonte, The Velvet Mafia boys, Ron Bass, Lidia Yuknavitch, Stella Hershan, Andi Olsen, Marc Lowe.

Special Thanks to Ralph Berry, Lance Olsen, Carmen Edington, Dan Waterman, Lou Robinson, and everyone at FC2 and the University of Alabama Press who helped make this book into the object you are holding in your hands.

And to the extraordinary Joachim Schwabe, creator of the infamous Überfisch: words cannot sufficiently express my gratitude.